AHMED MA

To Merilyn & Joyce &
to Palestine, your memory
& my presence.

VANISHED

THE MYSTERIOUS DISAPPEARANCE

OF MUSTAFA OUDA

love,
Ahmad
8/3/19

A NOVEL

RIMAL PUBLICATIONS

masoud.ahmad@gmail.com

First published in 2015
Reprinted 2016

Rimal Publications,
Cyprus
www.rimalbooks.com

ISBN 978-9963-715-13-8

ACKNOWLEDGEMENTS

There are many people to thank for their invaluable advice and help. Immense gratitude goes out to Heather Gardner, Rebecca Sowray, Anne Hartnoll, Hicham Yaza, Karyn Dougan, Lisa Van Wyk, Cate Myddleton-Evans and Souraya Ali.

The biggest thank you goes to my family and friends in Gaza, who have been wonderful in providing some of the stories related in this book and for answering the endless questions about life in the 1970s and beyond.

The famous tales of *Kalila Wa Dimna* are often referred to in this book. They are originally ancient Indian tales known as the Panchatantra. They were translated into Arabic by the famous Persian scholar Abdullah Ibn El-Muqaffa in 750 CE, and have become an important part of the Arabic culture, much like the *One Thousand and One Nights*.

To my brave fellow Palestinians who have devoted their lives in the search for dignity and freedom

To my parents, my lovely wife Heather Gardner and our delightful two children Zino and Serene

1

"I have to go my love, the house has just been hit and phone lines are not connecting."

He was sitting on the long dark blue sofa, in the half-lit living room of their tiny two-bedroom flat on Clerkenwell Road. Smoke coming from his untouched cigarette was penetrating her nose as she stood half-dressed by the main door near the open-plan kitchen. Her wide dark brown eyes were hardly visible, only the white skin of her legs glowed in the dark, down her mini shorts, which she often used as pyjamas on hot summer evenings in London. Zoe stood there not knowing what to say, she kept watching her husband bending down, head touching his knees, dressed in a black top and blue tracksuit bottoms, his dark olive skin blending with the colour of the room.

"Get in the shower, I will pack a few things for you," she whispered so as not to wake up their son.

He knew this was coming at some point, that tiny house in Gaza wouldn't be able to stand the heavy bombardment for a long time. Every evening, Omar came home from work in a hurry to switch on the Al Jazeera *news channel to catch up with the latest news. He would kiss Mustafa quickly without paying attention to all the requests of a four-year-old to play superhero games or read him a story. His social life had almost fallen apart due to all the events regularly arranged around Mustafa's circle of friends. Even then, he only exchanged the necessary words with other parents, filling the conversation with talks about expensive nursery fees and the warm few weeks this July and exchanging tips on books and games that keep children entertained. But deep inside, Omar was absent, worried sick about everyone in Gaza and angry with himself for being so far away, frustrated every time he couldn't get through over the phone.*

He broke down when his Uncle Attiya phoned and asked to be forgiven for all the mistakes he had made. Omar did not know what to say, listening away to his uncle's deep voice mixed with the sound of explosions in the background. Sobs filled his throat as he tried to tell his uncle to stay strong, to pray that things would be over soon. He did not expect it to last so long and hoped that the tiny house would stay safe. But it wasn't just the house that troubled him, it was the story hidden in its thin walls, the story of a boy growing up in fear and later the reconciliation that finally happened there and allowed him to let go and move on, start a new life in London. Omar couldn't sleep before reading all the news articles and live Twitter updates on his phone. The first thing he did when he woke up was read the news again. He wasn't sure what he was going to wake up to.

Omar continued to go to work, walking in silence every day from his flat to the office near Angel Tube Station, listening to online Gaza radio stations streaming local songs on his phone. He would greet his colleagues warmly and immediately engage in the typical English conversation about the weather. Omar enjoyed this distraction and the support he received from everyone in his eight-people-strong team. His cigarette breaks, however, became more frequent, finger flicking through his phone, texting friends in Gaza and his Uncle Attiya to make sure they were still ok. He would go back to his desk and send a few emails, keeping on top of everything as a way of distracting himself. On his way back, he looked pensive through the rush hour as people walked very quickly, trying to catch the bus or rushing to a pub. The streets of London were always too busy to allow him to immerse himself in thoughts analysing what was going on while hoping that a ceasefire would be implemented soon and the whole nightmare would be over.

But it all happened that night on July the 30th and he learned about it through Twitter just before midnight. It was time to go back home, even though it was almost impossible to do so.

"I will call you from Cairo and then as soon as I get into Gaza." He was drying his hair as he stood naked in front of her in their dark bedroom while she handed him his Palestinian and British passports.

"Why don't you wait a little bit, maybe you will be able to connect to your uncle and find out more?"

"I need to go, at least I could bring back that photograph." He paused, thinking of that moment when both he and Zoe hung up the photo frame on the cracked wall in the middle of the room in the Jabalia Camp before kissing his uncle goodbye and heading to the Rafah Border Crossing on the way to London.

Omar went through the tiny corridor leading from their bedroom to the second small single room to see Mustafa deep in sleep. He put his T-shirt on and bent down to kiss him goodbye. He stared at every single corner of their flat which they furnished together. It looked smaller. He needed to get going, there was nothing in Omar's mind apart from getting into Gaza. He had already confirmed that there was a seat available on the 7:45am BA flight to Cairo.

The Afghan refugee driver was talking non-stop all the way to the airport as the mini cab almost flew on the A40 and M25 roads, telling Omar how he escaped the war in Afghanistan, describing his journey to Europe and his eventual arrival in the UK. But Omar wasn't really listening, he just stared out of the window, head leaning on the glass, eyes fixed on the headlights of the other cars. He was tempted to open the door and throw himself out, letting go of everything, ending what seemed to be an ill-fated life, thinking that it could all be over if he just opened the door and let himself out.

But the door was only opened by the driver when they got to Terminal 3 at Heathrow Airport, which was busy with parents and wide-awake children making lots of noise, excited about their holidays. Just before he boarded the plane, Omar's phone rang.

"Baba, it's me Mustafa, wain inta, *where are you?"*

"I am at the airport, Mama must have told you I am going to Gaza, Inshallah,*" his voice shaking as he said the words. "God willing."*

"I want to come with you, I miss Gaza."

"Not now son, it's too dangerous. Be a good boy and listen to what Mama says."

"Why are you going if it is too dangerous then?" The innocence of a four-year-old made Omar stop.

"I am a superhero remember? Don't worry about me, I will fight the baddies off. I'll tell you what, I will bring you a present, what do you want?"

"Batmobile."

"OK, bye Mustafa, deer balak, *take care of yourself."*

"Bye Baba."

"Take care of yourself my love," Zoe grabbed the phone, "and keep me posted, I will be thinking of you."

"I will, and you look after yourself habeebti.*" He hung up wondering when would be the next time he would see them, or whether he would ever see them again. Suddenly, he felt sick. What if anything happened to him? Would Mustafa ever understand? Would he really get why his dad left his comfortable life in London along with his wife and his only child to go back to a war zone in search of rubble and a photograph? Would Zoe tell him everything as he would've liked her to tell him? Tears filled his eyes. Everyone at the gate stared at him. A six-year-old girl came close and offered him some tissues which he accepted with a smile. Holiday makers, journalists and businessmen in scruffy suits seemed to have stopped their conversation and fixed their eyes on this 33-year-old man standing and crying like a little child.*

Despite his well-built physique, wide chest and shoulders, he *looked no more than a three-year-old longing to go home. Omar went straight to the BA desk to ask how long he had left before he could board and immediately turned around and started running towards the duty free zone. He found a WH Smith, picked up a thick leather notebook and a pen and then jumped the queue to pay before heading back to the gate as fast as he could. To his relief, there were a couple of people still queuing to get on.*

As soon as he sat on his aisle seat, he opened the brand new notebook and started writing:

> *My Dearest Mustafa,*
>
> *I am not sure where to start from. One day you will grow up and you may never need to read this because we will be together and I will tell you the whole story myself. But in case anything happens to me, I wanted to explain why I left so suddenly without waking you up, why this journey is very important to me and why this house had a story that you may want to know fully. Your mum will no doubt explain everything to you, but I wanted you to hear it from me as well. So here it is, in full. I tell it with all honesty so you may one day look back and continue to think of me as a superhero. Do what you like with it, bury it, burn it or tell it to others. It's now yours. I spent my whole life wondering where my father was, and I don't want the same to happen to you.*
>
> *This should tell you a lot about my childhood and the 30 years of my life that followed. It all started when I was eight years old in 1989, stupidly deciding to play a detective, determined to find your grandfather. I leave it to you to judge whether I was a coward or not, but please remember that I had no choice in all of this. I*

was stupid and made terrible mistakes, whose impact I thought was over. But now that my, and your, house has been destroyed, they have all come to the surface again.

There's no postal service in Gaza, but I will make sure it gets to you before I get there.

With all my love and prayers for reuniting with you very soon.

Yours,

Dad

2

My father was gone. I was too young to understand why, and nobody was able to explain it to me, not even my mother. When I asked she would always give me a sad smile, unlike her usual watermelon grin. I hated it when she did that. It frightened me. There was danger in that smile, which I could not understand, a hidden story that I was desperate to uncover. But she never told me, despite my desperate attempts to make her talk. Perhaps this is what pushed me to proclaim myself the youngest detective in the Jabalia Camp at the age of eight.

I learnt not to talk about my father. Sometimes I missed him so much, almost as if I had nails growing in my heart. However hard Mum tried to make it better for me, there was a hole in the middle of the family where Dad should have been. An empty space whenever we sat down to eat, a place that couldn't be filled by anyone else. Everybody had a father except me and it hurt, but nobody wanted to know, no one listened when I tried to explain how much I missed him. But for one last time, I wanted to hear the scripted story from her so I could take it from there. Although I was eight years of age, there was so much destruction around me it forced me to grow up much faster. Or maybe I believed I did.

One February morning in 1982, seven months after I was born, Mother woke up and found our front door unlocked, a warm small cup of sage tea perfuming the salty air. It was still dark outside, which made the house look even smaller. Realising there had been a power cut, she searched for a candle and lit it. She opened the front door and looked around the narrow alley with patriotic graffiti on its walls. Sometimes Israeli soldiers forced the men in the Jabalia Camp to come out in the middle of the night to clean off the graffiti and the anti-occupation slogans, painted on the outside walls by Palestinian freedom fighters. Everyone in the camp had to have gallons of white spirit and several brushes stored in their houses to be prepared for such occasions, as they never knew when the masked men would come to paint it or when the Israeli soldiers would take notice and order its removal.

During the three years of their marriage, Mother would often watch Father erase from the walls of the camp a white pigeon stuck behind prison bars and carrying an olive twig in its beak, or the Palestinian flag with its red triangle at the top and black, white and green strips coming out of it.

"Don't say anything, Mustafa, please," she would whisper in his ears as the heavily-armed soldiers barged into their bedroom in the middle of the night, pointing their guns at both their faces. Mother always wore a long black embroidered dress to bed in case the men came in the night. She kept a headscarf by her mattress on the badly tiled floor in case the soldiers walked in unexpectedly. Some nights she just slept wearing it.

Father, however, enjoyed sleeping in his boxer shorts. He would enjoy the shock on the soldiers' faces as he lifted up his covers, standing up as slowly as he could, yawning loudly, stretching his arms in the air then pulling a cigarette out from the drawer of the side table where he had a lighter placed on top. Their room was much smaller than mine and had one side table, dresser drawers with a big mirror, a small old olive wood wardrobe, but no bed. They slept on two mattresses on the floor that were often stored in my big room and taken out only at night. Mother continued this practice even after Father disappeared.

"Pass me the lighter, will you?" he would ask whoever was closest to the table. Very often the soldier would be confused and look towards their boss who was doing all the shouting, ordering my father to hurry up. Sometimes a soldier obeyed Father's orders, which pleased him enormously.

"Souad, when they are in my bedroom, I am in control," he would laugh, a deep and loud guffaw uttered whenever Mother would talk to him about not making fun of the soldiers.

"One day they will be angry with you and you will regret it."

"Or maybe they will stop coming and save us and themselves the humiliation."

Sometimes this would turn into an argument between the two of them, with Mother ending up refusing to speak to him or sometimes not serving tea to his mates when they came to visit. This made Father angry as it undermined his social status, as wives were expected to carry on with their household duties regardless of what was happening in the household. Father never shouted or raised his voice at her. Instead, he would refuse to speak to Mother for a while and end up doing his socialising elsewhere, normally in the local café with the other men, smoking lots of shisha on the side. He would stay there for a long time, not to annoy her but to avoid more arguments, which normally ended when she cooked a nice meal and things got talked through.

She was 24 years old in 1979, and although six years younger than him, she was still considered to be too old for marriage by Gaza's standards. Most girls in the late '70s got married at 19 and no older. People talked about Mother being too arrogantly beautiful and too fussy in choosing a husband. She was pale-skinned and tall, with thick straight black hair and wide blue eyes. When my grandfather took my father to ask for her hand in marriage, her response was: "He is the one I have been waiting for."

They were then engaged for a year, which added to her already damaged reputation. But Mother didn't care; she was madly in love with Father and could have easily been engaged to him forever, enjoying the journeys my father took her on and the places they visited together.

The 45-minute drive from Jabalia to Khan Younis in the south always depressed her, and as she leaned her head on the passenger window of Father's old 1952 rusty Mercedes, she wished that it would break down so that they could take a walk out in the country, gazing at the olive groves that stretched between Al-Nusairat, Deir El-Balah and Khan Younis. She had a favourite spot that she used to go to as a teenager when she ran away from school, just after the turning from the Salah El-Dein main road, which runs through the entire Gaza Strip, towards Deir El-Balah.

In the early '70s, as a girl, she would climb a small sandy hill that always had litter at the bottom of it and roll cigarettes with a couple of schoolmates. They would stay there until an hour before school finished, giving themselves enough time to return home without any of their fathers suspecting anything. They would laugh and tease each other and gaze at the vast sea in the distance, seeing Israeli gunboats floating on the water. Sometimes, Israeli military jeeps would stop and search them, asking for ID cards. They would beg not to be arrested so that their families wouldn't find out what they had been up to. Mother was not that scared; she often wanted to be arrested, challenging the soldiers to do so, to the dismay of her mates who would beg her to be quiet. Sometimes the soldiers would just sit with them and smoke cigarettes too. After all, they were only teenagers.

That day in February, she closed the front door but left it unlocked, stepping back slowly into the dark house and walking through the narrow corridor. Father was not cleaning graffiti. She peaked into the bathroom to double check if he was there before putting out the candle and slipping under her duvet. Apparently, I was curled up on her mattress in deep sleep. She kissed me on my chubby seven-month-old cheeks before falling asleep again.

I had heard this story often, but every time Mother recounted it to me she just looked past me. Our eyes never met. I was too small to understand what that look meant. It was almost like she felt guilty for going back to sleep and not going out after Father. Often guilt overcame me, too, for falling asleep that night and for not making any sound to wake up Mother.

I made Mother recount the same story many times, but still it did not make sense. Why would Father disappear like that? Was he arrested, killed, ran away? Mother never offered any answer. By the time I was eight years old, able enough to go out by myself, it was time to launch my own investigation and to go on a trail that nearly killed me, chasing a shadow with very little evidence. The only clue available was a marriage certificate, dated September 3rd 1979, which named Father and Souad El-Henawi, a lawful couple. My name appeared on a blue UN Refugee Family Card, showing my parents' names and details in a long landscape table on the reverse, and on which my name and date of birth, 13 July 1981, was a handwritten addition. It was signed and dated by the UN Refugee caseworker six months after I was born; almost a week after Father disappeared. These papers became stained and crumpled with time, like a small creature that had been asleep at the bottom of Mother's dressing drawer, hidden yet brought back to life every time I pulled them out to reread the details and remind myself that I had a father. There was also a key of our home in the village of Deir Suneid, now part of Israel.

There were no photographs of Father anywhere in the house. The walls stood mostly bare, except for a few framed Quran verses and white paint peeling off the corners, forming a shore-like line. The grey asbestos sheets, which stood on top of the cracked walls to form a roof, made our two, small, bedroom house on Sanaida Street even paler. My room stood at the end of the house overlooking a small alley to the left across from which Um Marwan's house stood. I would stand at my window for hours sometimes, watching passers-by, kids coming home with their parents, fathers lifting their children on their shoulders or telling their young ones off for getting their clothes dirty. Standing there watching the world go by made me feel very small. The house was not big; it could hardly accommodate more than six people at one time. But when playing hide-and-seek games with Mother, or pacing up and down the corridor, wondering where my father was, or when running away afraid my uncle would punish me, the house felt big enough for my small body to dodge its corners and find hiding places.

The house was in the Jabalia Camp, on the northeast side of the Gaza Strip, a dirty place with no paved roads. Most of the houses were built without planning permission and they stuck out in different shapes and sizes, making our street an assortment of houses of all sorts. The camp, like so many others, was meant to be temporary, following the events of 1948. But through the years it transformed to more permanent structures, with brick walls and mostly asbestos-sheet roofs.

Every day I walked along littered streets, where even golden sand that covered the street always looked dirty, to Al-Fakhoura Primary School for Boys. Sometimes I would pick fruit from the few small fig trees that were scattered along Sanaida Street. My journey took me past Abu Mohammed's house and down to the water pump, where a small square and a side road led to El-Hawaja Street. Men were often scattered on the side of the road, sometimes playing backgammon, or smoking shisha.

Walking past Abu Rashid's Water Reservoir on El-Hawaja Street, the smell was so horrible I had to pinch my nose so hard it left a red mark for the rest of the day. It was as if an entire animal population had died in there. That smell was quickly replaced by jasmine and mint as I walked up El-Hawaja Street and turned right onto El-Shuhada Square to go to school.

Here the stark landscape was momentarily relieved by a couple of farms that had lots of trees and herbs that were sold at the local market. Sometimes I stood there for a long time before continuing to school, or before heading back home to get shouted at by Mother or Uncle Attiya. The truth was that I loved school because it took my mind off home and off thinking about Father.

On the way back from school, my daily ritual was to stop and chat to our neighbour Um Marwan who lived in the house opposite ours, separated only by a small nameless alley. I enjoyed our conversations and I learned a lot about Father in the absence of more facts from Mother. Often I would get back from school and find Um Marwan sitting on a small ripped mattress outside her front door, gazing at the street. She would see me walking down the small slope at the top of the street and would wave. Her usual black, stained dress hardly covered her old legs and their network of varicose veins. Sweets were always ready, tucked away in a small crumpled black plastic bag. Sometimes, Mother would see us on her way out of Uncle Attiya's house and would smile without saying hello, the same scary smile she gave me when Father was mentioned. I never understood why Mother didn't want me to speak to Um Marwan, or why this neighbour was never invited to our house.

Um Marwan would smile as she tucked a handful of brown buttery sweets wrapped in purple foil into my pocket and ask, "Are you going to be an educated man like your father?" She always had sweets, even on non-Eid days. She told me how much respect everyone had for Father. He was the most educated man in the whole of the neighbourhood, with a Masters in Arabic Literature from Cairo University at a time when most people around him rarely finished high school. People always called him *Ustaz,* "teacher", even though he had never taught in schools. Still, this was the most respectable job a man could have.

Father worked in a small translation office, translating legal documents into Arabic, English and Hebrew. Um Marwan told me that people would come to him for advice on everything – asking which school to send their children to or to read doctors' notes or to ask him to translate an Israeli evacuation order from Hebrew. Sometimes men would even come to ask for his advice regarding their emotional problems with their wives. Father never refused any request and it amused him to know so much about people. Um Marwan told me how she had never seen Father walking down the street by himself.

"The moment Mustafa stepped out of that door, someone would pounce on him to ask for something or invite him over for lunch," She would sigh as if he was her long lost lover, even though she was at least sixty years old.

Um Marwan had lived in the same spot since the *Nakba* of 1948. She had arrived with her husband, Abu Marwan, in Jabalia after Israel completely destroyed their village of Herbia, which was on the outskirts of Jerusalem. She and all her family had fled their village that day, going wherever they could find refuge, and for years Father tried to help her locate her parents and siblings. He would write letters on her behalf and send them to local radio stations in Jordan, Lebanon, Syria and Egypt, in the hope that one day someone would respond to her. She would wait by the radio every Tuesday morning, sipping a small cup of thick, black, cardamom coffee. She often kicked her husband out so she could listen carefully to the radio, held in both hands, eyes looking at the speaker as if someone was about to jump out and embrace her. Her wrinkled olive-skinned face would relax as she put her tattooed hand over it and waited for the letters to be read on air.

"No news is good news," my father always told her. "We will write more letters and maybe one day we can put an advert in the local papers too."

Um Marwan saw in Father the younger brother she once had. When my father wanted to ask for Mother's hand in marriage, she even went with my grandfather and sat with the men when they asked for Mother's hand in marriage. Everyone was surprised to see her there, especially given that she wasn't even part of the family. But no one could have stopped her. She begged my grandfather to allow her to go with them and threatened to bad-mouth father, by claiming that she was his secret lover, if she wasn't allowed to go.

She did not go to Mother's hen party, as was the custom of all women. Instead, she read the first verse of the Quran with the rest of the men in August as part of the engagement ceremony and danced outside in the street at Father's bachelor party that September of 1979. Father enjoyed her company a lot and listened to her stories with intensity, which often flattered her. She always told him the same story of how she and her family were forced to leave their homes in 1948. Father kept silent as she recounted the events and told of how she looked for somewhere safe, knowing her daughter might die of the cold.

After my grandfather died, when I had only been in Mother's womb for a few weeks, Father and his brother, Uncle Attiya, decided to divide the big house into two sections. Father's share was the smallest but he didn't mind. He wasn't planning to have a large family anyway. He always said that living in the Jabalia Refugee Camp was just temporary and he was going to return to our original home in Deir Suneid one day. Uncle Attiya built the biggest house in the whole of the Jabalia Camp with his big share, with lots of lemon and apricot trees and a vine. In springtime, people would stop outside the walls of his house just to fill their noses with a waft of the blossoms. Um Marwan told me how Father was very happy with his share. He built the two-bedroom house on his own, even though he had no prior experience of construction work. But it never made sense to me that Father would accept a smaller share of the house, why Mother and I had to be squashed in a tiny place when Uncle lived in what felt like a villa.

Um Marwan never visited us even though I invited her many times. One warm spring day in April 1989, I literally dragged her in but she only stayed a few minutes before she excused herself. I begged her to stay for dinner while Mother remained silent. Um Marwan protested and made faint excuses that she hadn't informed anyone that she was eating outside.

"I could go and tell Abu Marwan," I spoke hastily pleading for her to stay.

"No, I must go." She started putting her shoes on and was about to fall over when she quickly grabbed her old brown walking stick and leaned on it.

"This house is cursed," I heard her mutter under her breath as she rushed out.

Mother was smiling; she walked up to me and wrapped my body with her big hug.

"Don't worry about her, she is the cursed one."

She gave me a kiss on the cheek and continued to look and smile at me. I felt very small in her arms; she was a tall woman and had a strong grip. She was dressed nicely that day, with tight jeans and a white top underneath her long black *jilbab* dress. As I brushed my hand over her thick straight black hair, tracing its flow over her shoulders, I noticed something different.

"You're wearing glasses?"

"Yes, I have had them for a while but never wore them outside my bedroom. They are for reading really."

She turned around and headed for the kitchen, which was at the other end of the house, as I continued to watch her, amazed at how beautiful she looked. She was only thirty-four years old in 1989 although she looked much younger. She pushed me aside and closed the metal door that led straight to the living room.

I had a small black and white passport-size photo of my father tucked in one of my schoolbooks, which I carried with me every day. I always told myself that I would save up to buy a wallet for the photograph, but whenever I failed, I convinced myself that maybe it was for the best and that it was a sign that Father was coming back.

By the time I was eight years old, neither had happened, instead I kept changing the location of the picture from one book to the other or into my pockets, making sure it was always with me. Father was my invisible companion. I often stared at his wide eyes, which I was convinced were green, his thick black curly hair, wide forehead and thick wide lips open slightly over bright teeth.

Sometimes I thought he could see me as he stared out of the picture. I could only see his shoulders and wondered whether he could lift me up in one move or not. What was going on in his mind as he posed for the photograph? He was wearing what looked like a dark pair of jeans and a shirt as was fashionable at the time; it made me smile to think of my own dad as a fashionable guy who kept up to date with the latest trends. His hair was dark and curly, just like mine. His straight pointy nose and olive skin gave him a gentle look; something I was pleased to inherit as it made me look like a miniature version of him. I looked at this man, the man I resembled and longed to know how he could disappear overnight without a trace.

Every time I opened my book to look at his photograph, I imagined Father talking to me, telling me how much he missed me, his voice loud, gravelly from too many cigarettes. I imagined him standing by the window, sunlight dusting his tired features.

3

A good detective cannot do his job properly without the help of a sidekick. I learned that through the endless series of Egyptian crime books for children about a boy called Takhtakh who kept an eye on criminals in his neighbourhood and reported them to the police. There was no candidate who would be up for the job apart from my best friend Ahmed. One day, I decided to walk to his house in the northern side of Jabalia Camp to tell him of my mission, tucking the official papers and Father's photograph into the front of my pocketless trousers and covering them with my green T-shirt. My mission was to employ him to find more information about the house. He was to find out why we ended up with such a small share. Tracing Father's footsteps was my responsibility.

It had rained that evening and the smell of the warm walls penetrated my nostrils as I walked through the narrow streets, which were filled with puddles. The smell of moss and charcoal filled the air. The small alleys were empty as usual; people stayed at home to keep out of the cold evening after the rain had swept away the warmth of the morning sun. When I got to El-Hawaja Street, I realised that cold wasn't the only thing that kept people inside. The busy road that was normally full of stall sellers – filling the air with the smell of freshly fried falafel or roasted sweet corn, with kids playing and men sitting outside on small chairs, playing cards and drinking coffee while puffing so many cigarettes – was deserted. There was a curfew.

I had forgotten the announcement coming from the speakers on the military jeep earlier that day in our street. It was now 6pm, which meant there was fourteen hours before it would be lifted. I saw flashing lights in the distance and stayed nailed to the ground, huddled down like a deflated ball. Out of the corner of my eye, I saw a soldier walking towards me, gun in hand. I started to shake, not knowing what to do. There was no way back, the soldier would see me move and chase me back through the alleys. What would Mother or Uncle Attiya say? I would be sure to get a hard time for doing such a stupid thing. Just then, I looked back and saw the tall silhouette of a masked man, wrapped in a Palestinian *kufiyyah* scarf, dressed in a black top, a puffer jacket, which failed to hide his big belly, and sky blue jeans. He was standing in the corner a few alleys away from me. It was too dark to see well, but I knew his eyes were fixed on me. His features were hidden underneath the mask he wore, but for some reason he looked familiar, as if we had met before. It was too dark to see his eyes closely, but the way he stared made me feel I was in the company of someone who knew me well. How long had he been there? I kept looking at him, hoping he would be able to help me. But he turned around and started walking away along the long dirty lane, water splashing violently as his boots met the puddles.

At the end of the street, I watched as he put his hand in his back pocket, pulled something out and then raised his arm in the air and fired. The sound of the shot made me shout, but I quickly recovered, putting my hand on my mouth so as not to attract the soldier. There was a moment of silence before I heard car engines driving fast down El-Hawaja Street. From the corner of the street I saw flashlights fade away and the sound of sirens seemed less audible. At the age of eight, it was the first time I had heard the sound of live ammunition from such a small distance. It paralysed me momentarily, and then I started pinching myself to make sure I was still alive.

I ran quickly past Abu Rashid's Water Reservoir and lodged myself into a nearby shed, waiting before moving on through more small alleys until I finally got to the Abu Hussein Primary School, behind which Ahmed's big house stood dark and quiet. I took a deep breath, cursing about how many small alleyways Jabalia had.

There was no electricity by the time I got there and the street was pitch black, making me trip on a stone in the street, falling head first into a big puddle. I started knocking on the metal sheet door as violently as I could, hoping someone would open before the soldier found me standing in the street. Murmurs started in the house, Ahmed's father's deep voice came through, asking who was there but I didn't dare respond. They probably thought it was the soldiers. At first when he opened the door, he looked over my head – I was too small for his big body. He was dressed in a big thick grey *jalabiya*, with another gown-like layer that trailed on the floor. In the darkness, I saw his hand move up to his thick beard, scratching it as he looked down to me, eyes glowing in the dark.

"Omar, what are you doing here?" His voice trembled and he looked very worried.

"Is Ahmed here?"

"Yes, come in before anyone sees you in the street, quick." He put his hand on my right shoulder and ushered me inside, pulling my entire body forward, quickly shutting the door behind. He guided me through the open-air courtyard before reaching their guest room, which was cold and dark.

"Soumaya, bring a candle to the guest room please," he shouted at the top of his voice so that his daughter could hear him from the other end of the house.

Ahmed came carrying a candle in his right hand and guarding it with his left palm so it would not blow out.

"*Ahlan wa Sahlan* Omar, welcome. What brings you here at this time? Is everything all right?"

His father was watching impatiently, waiting for the answer but I didn't know what to say. I had intended to have a quiet chat with my friend and not this unexpected scene.

"I… I was out visiting a cousin nearby and got caught in the curfew. I can't go home, too many soldiers on the road."

I did not want to admit the real reason I came to see Ahmed. People avoided visiting each other in the evenings because of the curfews. Arriving in such a dramatic manner scared Ahmed's family and made them think that there was an emergency somehow. I saw Ahmed's father sigh in relief. He had thought the worst.

"I will leave you to it; let's hope the curfew will be lifted in the morning as they said. Does your mother know that you are here?"

"No." I looked away as I said it, feeling guilty about not telling Mother where I was going. She must be worried sick.

"Okay, well she will have a hard time sleeping tonight, but everything will be alright in the morning. We will get you home first thing or find a way to tell her that you are here. I will send some blankets for you two to sleep in this room. Are you hungry?"

"No."

"Very well, then. Goodnight."

"Abu Ahmed?" I called him "Father of Ahmed" as was the tradition of respecting elders. We never used adults' first names when addressing them in public. A big part of me wished to hear people call Father, Abu Omar.

"Yes?"

"Thanks for letting me stay, and sorry to disturb you like this."

"It's all right, my friend," Ahmed responded quickly. "You would do the same for me. We all do. That's one thing the Israelis can't stop us from doing, I can tell you that." His father smiled as he exited while Ahmed felt proud about what he had said. It felt like a line he had heard before and repeating it gave him a sense of importance.

Soumaya, Ahmed's older sister, brought us some blankets and a very sweet tea, which I drank with delight as he prepared our bedding, rearranging the guest mattresses on the floor to turn them into a bed. We settled into bed after changing into some of Ahmed's pyjamas. He was very sleepy and ready to fall into deep sleep almost instantly.

"You should be proud of your father."

I stared at the ceiling as I spoke, wondering what it would feel like to come home and find Father waiting for me at home, worried about my absence, opening the door for me just as Abu Ahmed did. A small child standing in front of him, looking for protection.

"I am," he said while stretching his mouth wide and letting out a big yawn.

"I wish I could have been as lucky as you are." Silence fell after I said that. My friend didn't know what to say. "I want to find him Ahmed. I need you to help me."

My friend did not reply, already breathing deeply. I blew out the candle and pulled the covers tight over my head, but I could not sleep for a long time. I kept staring at my friend. When we woke up in the morning, the sun had come out again, drying up the sandy streets of Jabalia. The sound of street vendors told us that the curfew had been lifted. I could hear the children playing in the yard of Abu Hussein School, and it took me a moment to realise both Ahmed and I were extremely late for school.

His father brought us some falafel sandwiches that smelt delicious. The sizzling hot oil burnt my tongue as I quickly shoved the sandwich inside my mouth while at the same time trying to put my shoes on. Ahmed took his time getting up, wandering to the bathroom to brush his teeth while I hovered by the door scoffing the rest of the sandwich. He looked completely refreshed by the time he reappeared, smiling as I scowled at him. Mother would be worried about me.

On the street, I started running as quickly as I could while Ahmed zigzagged his way through the muddy roads. He wanted to come with me to prove to Mother that I had stayed with him the night before and that I hadn't been anywhere she wouldn't approve of.

"What is it you were saying about your father last night? Of course I will help you find him, silly." My heart almost stopped as his words penetrated my ears, glad that my sidekick has accepted the job. We walked back slowly, hatching a plan of where to start looking for him. Occasionally, Ahmed would look at me and ask "what if..." and I would interrupt him immediately, snapping at him that Father was still alive. I was convinced of it.

We made a list of people to interview, including his old boss at the translation office, our neighbour Um Marwan and some of his other friends who used to live a few streets away from us. The one candidate we really wanted to question was the Israeli military general, Uri, who was stationed in the Jabalia Refugee Camp, but that would be difficult. He was based in El-Markaz Military Station in the heart of the camp and when he came out, terror often spread throughout the streets. He suspected everyone of being a freedom fighter, making them a legitimate target of his abuse. Old men, children, women; no one escaped his anger. Two years had passed since the beginning of the first *Intifada* and Uri was responsible for shooting many people on our street. How was I to even approach such a man?

It took several months before I could muster up the courage to go to El-Markaz to speak to Uri. I would wait on the main street for a long time staring at the walls that were smothered in barbed wire, with shards of glass scattered along the top. The main building was far from the front wall with thick metal windows and tinted glass. There were snipers permanently stationed at the watchtowers.

My whole body would tremble the moment the guns would

turn towards my direction, knowing the spyglass of the sniper was targeting me, not being able to see whether the soldier's finger was on the trigger or not. I would back off immediately then, cursing myself for failing and feeling very unworthy of the mission I had set myself on.

Ahmed and I would update each other at school on our separate investigations. During the break we would walk together to the canteen, hands in pockets, and chat about it while looking ahead so as not to draw any attention to what we were doing. We didn't want anyone to know about our activities and avoided talking about the subject at each other's houses. Our visits had become less frequent anyway, since most evenings we had errands to run. Ahmed told me he was going to see some of Father's friends to talk to them, while I tried to stay at home to get Mother to tell me more. She never did and I always wondered why. Was she also trying to find him? Or did she know what had happened but refused to tell me?

One hot Friday morning, a week before my ninth birthday, I woke with a headache having spent the night thinking about how to approach Uri. I received a scolding from Mother for getting up late, she wanted me to go and get some ingredients from the market to cook the fish she had bought the day before. She needed lemons, mint and cumin for her recipe. I hurried into the street, passing people preparing for the Friday prayer; freshly showered kids looking unusually clean; lots of men in white *jalabiya* gowns; and women returning from the market burdened with black plastic bags. Some of the houses already smelled of boiled meat, even though it was still morning. I bought what I needed from the market and walked back on my now usual route that ran by El-Markaz.

I followed the cars quickly and entered through the main gate just as it was about to be shut. The moment I was on the other side, I heard the sound of a gun being loaded and someone shouting in

Hebrew: "*Taatsour.* Stop. *Tarim yadayem.* Hands Up." The plastic bags rustled as my hands shook. I froze, not knowing what to do, worried I was going to wet myself. The soldier repeated his orders to put my hands in the air. More soldiers came out of the building as I gently placed down the bags. I looked up and saw Uri standing by the main entrance of the building, his dark shades and blonde hair glowing in the sun. Two soldiers swiftly appeared in front of him, while a third put his arm on his shoulder and led the General inside. More sounds of guns being loaded. Waiting. Crying.

Eventually they pulled back and removed their helmets, took out their radios and said something I didn't understand. A few seconds later, a soldier I didn't even realise was there kicked me in the back while another handcuffed me as I lay sprawled on the ground. They pulled me up sharply and began dragging me to the main entrance to the building.

Inside, the dark, narrow corridors stank of dampness and I could hear men shouting in Hebrew. Without warning, I was pushed into an empty room. Although it was summer I shivered as I waited, handcuffed and frightened, for someone to return. I thought about the shopping bags and of Mother waiting for me to bring home her groceries.

It was a few hours before the door opened again and to my surprise it was Uri who entered. All the trouble and fear seemed justified; at last I had made it in front of him, just him, and I could ask him about Father. He removed his dark Ray-Ban shades as he closed the door behind him, brushing his long blonde hair back with his white-skinned hand, looking like a well-made Lego man. As he approached me, I had to strain my neck to keep eye contact. He was the tallest person I had ever seen in my life.

His dark green military suit looked clean and shiny. I could almost see my reflection in his polished black boots. As he got close, he pushed me to the wall and lifted me with one hand by my collar. The blue jeans I was wearing were already ripped. My sandals had fallen off somewhere in the courtyard while I was being dragged.

"WHO DO YOU WORK FOR?"

His voice rang in my ears.

"Work for?"

"Are you Fatah? Those bastards that think they will sweep us Israelis into the sea? Or PFLP? Or maybe even *Khamas*, eh?" He pronounced Hamas with a strong 'Kh' sound.

"I do not work for anyone." I could hardly get the words out of my mouth.

"Who sent you here?"

"No one… I swear by Allah, no one."

Then he dropped me and as I fell on the ground he kicked me in my stomach. My tears started again.

"I swear by Allah…I swear."

"So why are you here? Don't you know no one is allowed to come near without being summoned? What is in those shopping bags? Do you know how much it costs to keep those explosive experts on site?"

"I do not know. I did not know. I am sorry for the inconvenience; I will go and never come back."

"You think it is as easy as that?" A mean smile crossed his face.

"I do not know. I do not know. I just wanted…" I stopped, unwilling to say more. My stomach hurt. It was difficult to breathe.

"What do you want, boy?"

"My father."

"I am sorry?"

"He disappeared nine years ago."

He was silent, waiting for me to say more. As he waited, he leaned against the wall and shoved a cigarette into his mouth, taking a deep drag and letting out a thick cloud of smoke.

"I don't know where he is," I finally continued. "He just disappeared. I think you have him or at least know where he is, but I know that he is not dead."

"And how do you know that?"

"I can feel it." He laughed loudly. "What is your name boy?"

"Ouda. Omar Ouda. My father was called Mustafa." Uri looked at me closely, then slowly walked towards me again. I tensed my body, afraid he was going to hit me again.

"Look, we are not a charity here OK! We are not responsible if your father buggered off somewhere and left you. Who would blame him to leave this dump? I am sure he had his reasons."

"My father did not run away, all right!" I shouted but kept my gaze lowered, waiting for him to punish me for raising my voice.

"Look, I will let you go this time, but if I ever see your face anywhere near El-Markaz, you will wish you were never born."

He then put his shades on, opened the door and shouted to a soldier who came and dragged me out again. He took me to the main gate and opened a small door before kicking me out on the main street.

It was late afternoon by the time I started making my way home. There had been no point of asking for my shopping back. Mother would probably kill me anyway when I got home. I wondered what I should tell her. Then, up ahead, I noticed another masked man in the corner of the street opposite. Although I couldn't see his face, I was convinced he was the same man who distracted the soldiers that night of the curfew. When our eyes met, he turned around and disappeared. I immediately ran after him, intending to follow him, but he vanished. I suddenly had the uneasy feeling I was being watched. Unhappy with this thought, I quickly pushed it from my mind and hurried home.

Our front door was open when I got home in the afternoon. The street was quiet, as most people were napping after their big Friday lunch. Normally, the heat of the sun would sedate people for a few hours. To my relief, Mother wasn't home. I went to the fridge and got out a cold bottle of water and drank half of it in one gulp. I was delighted to find fresh bread on the kitchen counter, which I munched on as I headed to my room before slipping under my covers and falling asleep almost instantly.

4

I was awakened soon, however, by Uncle Attiya, who towered above me as I lay on my mattress. He was wearing dark brown trousers and a white cotton shirt through which I could see his big hairy belly. His big nose and small eyes looked very mean as he watched me waking up; his short curly hair looked shiny as if he had just splashed some water over it.

I opened my eyes fully and knew a storm of a scolding was about to be unleashed. Uncle Attiya looked furious. Mother stood next to him with a *kufiyyah* wrapped around her hair, her fringe poking through eager to escape the scarf. She must have been in a rush, I thought looking at her unusual level of dishevelment.

"Where the hell have you been?"

This time, he didn't look like he was telling me off just for Mother's sake. He seemed genuinely angry.

"The whole street has been looking for you, idiot. We left no stone unturned. Hospitals, mosques… Everywhere!"

I thought they surely left the El-Markaz stone unturned, otherwise they would not have asked me where I was. He then bent down towards me and slapped me hard across the face, the power of his palm made my nose bleed. I got up shouting and tried to run but he blocked the door. I was forced to cower on the other side of the room, curled with my head between my knees, while Uncle's large legs began their merciless assault. I sat on my bottom, put my head between my knees and waited for the kicks to come from all directions. Sometimes he would use his hand to hit me hard on the head. I wasn't sure whether Mother was watching or she had already left the room. If Father were here, this would not be happening. He wouldn't allow Uncle to beat me like that. Father would never do anything like this to me. His legs now tired, Uncle took his belt off and started beating me with it. I tried to escape again but he kicked me back to the same corner. I started shouting for Mother to come and help me.

"Mother…Mother, please I beg you."

The belt continued to bite my skin. Uncle was aiming at my face.

"Mother… please…I won't… I won't do it again."

But Mother never came back. I looked up into Uncle's furious face not understanding why he was so angry with me.

"Please Uncle, *khalas,* enough… By Allah I won't do it again, I promise you."

Uncle slowed down his beating, then bent down and grabbed my collar, pulling me into his face.

"This is the last time I see you in the street on your own, do you understand me? Next time you go out, even to school, my son Khalid will be with you to bring you home. But for now you are not going anywhere."

He dropped me, and satisfied I had learned my lesson, finally left me alone. He slammed the door shut behind him and began murmuring with Mother. I crawled back to my mattress, swallowing my tears as the carpet burned my knees. I let the silence swallow me. I wanted to be ignored. I wanted to be nobody. So there I was. Instead of being imprisoned by the Israelis, which would have at least given me some national honour, my life was to become confinement to my room, spending my days under house arrest.

It wasn't until late evening when I heard my door open and

saw Mother walk in. I pretended I was asleep. I didn't want to talk to her, she left me alone for the beating, she didn't even try to stop it. She crouched down by my mattress and gently touched the bruising on my face. Then she stroked my hair, and started to cry. The sound of her tears hurt more than my wounds and my anger. She kissed my cheek and whispered, "You are the love of my life." It was my fault that she was so sad. I had been stupid and selfish. Eventually she left the room, leaving me alone with my guilt.

Despite my fatigue, I lay there for a long time unable to sleep. I had a sudden, strong urge to abandon my mission of finding Father. Where was he? If he was still alive, why hadn't he made any contact with me? Was he not intrigued to meet me and see what I looked like? Whether I even looked like him? Um Marwan always said that I had his eyes and olive skin. It was then almost a year after my search for Father had started, my body was growing slowly, I was almost 140cm tall with wide shoulders, almost catching up with Ahmed's size. There was a small broken mirror shard in my room that I kept looking at as I held it in my right hand and Father's photograph in the left, comparing how we both looked. My curly hair, colour, shoulder, thick full lips, pointy nose and wide forehead all looked like small versions of his. It pleased me to think that one day I would grow up to be as strong as he looked in the photograph. And how different he looked from my monstrous Uncle!

Uncle Attiya was a very large man, with large cheeks, small black eyes and a big belly. He always wore dark shirts, often with missing buttons, showing his hairy flesh. He had long thin legs and a flat bottom. His eyebrows were thick, but his black hair was very straight. He combed it to the left side of his head most of the time. He always smelt of cigarettes and coffee, but he also had a lot of respect in the whole street. His deep laughter could be heard from a distance. People admired his big house and his wealth.

Our relationship had always been very formal; he rarely

interfered in any business between Mother and myself. However, sometimes she would use him to force me to do things or give me a lecture about morality and respecting elders, but other than that, she admitted she had never liked him. Mother always said that Uncle was too obsessed with his own life and family to care much about his missing brother's family. But to me, he was a man of contradictions. He was very strict with Mother and me, yet at the same time he would make sure to smile or wink at me as he gave me a hard time. Sometimes he would send his son Khalid for me, asking me to go and see him after beating me up. Once at his house, he would offer sweets and play with me or get me to watch television, which I did to avoid receiving another beating. The truth was that we had a formal relationship; I never wanted to get very close to him or his family for fear that he might take Father's position. I preferred to stay away and pay my respects whenever possible.

He had three children; Khalid, the eldest, never spoke to me apart from the normal greetings in front of everyone in the street. He was five years older than me and so we had nothing in common. The twins, Issam and his sister, Riham, were three years younger than me. They mostly kept to themselves, which meant they were often bullied by other kids. However, the bullies would stop the moment Khalid turned up. He had a reputation of beating the hell out of his sibling's bullies. Their mother and my mother were good friends. They often chatted together, and would keep each other company on market trips or while cooking.

Miriam was a short, round woman with a round nose and rosy cheeks. She had long eyelashes and always wore white headscarves. She smiled a lot and never seemed worried about anything. She was good company for Mother. But it was Uncle who came to visit us all the time and never allowed his wife to come to our house. Often he would send for Mother to come and help his wife cook or clean, especially when he had a lot of visitors at Eid, or if there was a problem between the neighbours on the street, which Uncle always interfered to mediate. People had a lot of respect for him and listened to what he had to say. Being a large man helped his image, which he tried to present as the *Mukhtar,* head of the whole street. Mother complained that he used her like a servant most of the time; on top of the cooking and cleaning, she would also have to babysit for Uncle and his wife whenever they went out to dine with one of their many friends – she was expected to do it, no matter what she had on.

When I was five years old, he taught me how to play backgammon and we used to have many long games outside his house, particularly during the summer when it was too hot to sit underneath those scorching asbestos sheets. During those games I questioned Uncle about Father but always received the same response. However, he did tell me a lot about Father's childhood and how he was good at playing with marbles, which they did on the very same street that I grew up on. He said that the other kids used to avoid playing with his brother because he was so good. He was an entrepreneur, selling the other kids back the marbles he had won from them. He was also skilled at making kites, and he would make money by making a bundle and selling them to the kids who couldn't make them.

Uncle Attiya never played in the street with Father as he was six years older than him. As he grew to be a young man, my grandfather decided to send him to work on a construction site in Israel to make some money. He would spend weeks there on the site, only coming back for a weekend to visit the family. Now he was a big contractor that most of Israeli construction companies relied on to bring in low-paid Palestinian workers. Since having children, he started going to work in Israel very early and came back late, just like the thousands of Palestinian workers who woke up with the first call of prayer at around 4am, carried their lunch in a plastic bag and rushed to the Erez Crossing to start their work.

Uncle Attiya brought many treats for his children from Israel – including computer games. His house was the first to have a TV and a video recorder. Sometimes he would invite all the kids in the street to watch a cartoon that he bought in a market in Haifa or a Bruce Lee film which we all loved. My cousin Khalid didn't agree with his father's practice and on the Eid he would charge the kids money to watch this film, turning his small bulky TV and VCR into a homemade cinema. Khalid would install a small curtain on their front door, put a chair outside and start charging the kids one Shekel per movie.

My job in the business was to sell refreshments when all the kids were crowded in the room staring at the TV. He gave me piles of nuts to pour into small handmade paper cups and charged half a Shekel each. Khalid always shared the profit of the sales with me even though I never bought the ingredients. He never shared the profits of the cinema business though.

It was Uncle Attiya who bought me my first school uniform; sky blue denim trousers and T-shirt with smart black shoes. He also bought my school backpack which had a big picture of a flying Superman on it, filled with beautiful pencils. Mother thanked him but later she said that she would rather he didn't because he was just showing off with his money. Financially, Mother and I were fine because, as she explained, social services had allocated us a monthly allowance. Plus we received aid from the United Nations Relief and Works Agency, like all refugees in Palestine. Mother was generous and bought me everything I needed, sometimes more than I thought we could afford. But then again, there were only two of us and she hardly spent any money on herself.

It was three days before Uncle finally allowed me to leave the house, accompanied by my cousin Khalid. I couldn't wait to get to school and see Ahmed. During our customary walk in the courtyard, I felt ashamed for failing in my mission not to get information from Uri. Ahmed, on the other hand, had been doing a lot of investigating, just as he had promised. He was excited to tell me he had seen Mr. Othman, Father's old boss at the translation office. Ahmed and Othman already knew each other. Othman's small office was the only place in the Jabalia Camp that had a photocopy machine and Ahmed had to visit frequently to photocopy legal documents for his father. Ahmed explained how at Friday prayer he had bumped into Othman at the mosque and had prayed next to him.

Othman was a very large bald man, with hair coming out of his nostrils. He always wore a stripy smart shirt leaving the top two buttons undone, showing a forest-like chest hair. His moustache and beard were very thin but dark against his white face and green eyes. The kids sometimes called him Osmali, because he looked exactly like a fat version of an Ottoman sultan. Having the name Othman, the Arabic for Ottoman, helped spread this nickname. Othman had been an old friend of Father's. They had studied Arabic literature together at Cairo University, and when Father decided to stay there for his Master's Degree, Othman decided to return to Gaza to start his business. He found a small shop on Sikka Road, which used to have the railway connecting Gaza to Egypt and Northern Palestine built during the British occupation. He converted the shop into offices and when Father returned to Gaza, his job was waiting for him. Father didn't take much convincing since he didn't want to go into teaching. He had never believed in the censored education system; everyone in Gaza studied the Egyptian curriculum without any reference to Palestine – as ordered by the Israelis. And so, he went to work for Othman.

Othman had seven children, three boys and four girls, all of whom were as big as he was. He wore small round reading glasses with a dirty black thread that went around his neck. He had an annoying habit of licking his lips before talking, as if they were always dry. I had had many conversations with him about Father and their time in Egypt. He told me how Father used to love walking on the Corniche by the Nile River while eating a full plate of traditional Egyptian Kushari, filled with lentils, spaghetti and hot chilli sauce. He used to make sure to listen to Fairuz's music in the morning and Egyptian Abdel Halim Hafez's music in the afternoon: That was his ritual. The first thing he would do when he woke up in the morning was to have a fresh cup of Arabic coffee, filling their tiny one-bedroom flat with the smell of cardamom coffee. He was always worried about the political situation in the Arab world, particularly in Cairo.

Father and Othman did not only study and discuss politics, they also spent many happy days at student parties and belly dancing clubs. The conversations with Othman would often cut off at this point even though I begged him to continue. I wanted to know everything about Father and these stories of lavishness made me smile, imagining Father there dancing and shaking his belly with all those women. At the very least, they distracted me from the idea of him stuck somewhere, unable to move or come back to his family.

I could never bring myself to ask Othman about my Father's disappearance. I relied too much on his happy stories of Father with his music and his coffee and his studying. Othman always told me this with a big smile on his face and a very deep laugh.

"You will understand later my son, not now, not now," he would say as I questioned him further; he would then put a few coins in my pocket and ask me to drop by more often so he could check on me. But Ahmed came with something that Othman never told me and I never understood why he has just now decided to tell Ahmed. He mentioned that Um Shadi, an old neighbour of ours who had now moved to Al-Nusairat, heard an argument in the house on the night before Father disappeared. When she looked out of her window, she saw Father slamming the door behind him and leave followed by Uncle Attiya.

Finally, proof that Mother and Uncle's story was not the entire truth. Something had happened, and they were not telling me.

Ahmed was watching me closely.

"Look perhaps there is some mistake," he said, trying to comfort me. "Who is Um Shadi anyway?"

"She used to be our neighbour. She moved to Al-Nusairat in the middle of the Strip."

"Well, we just have to go see her and ask her some questions," Ahmed said matter-of-factly.

My bodyguard Khalid came at the end of the school day to accompany me home as instructed by his father. We walked home in silence except for the occasional greetings to the familiar faces we passed. Um Marwan was sitting at her usual spot outside the house. She raised a hand when she saw us walk by, obviously understanding the awkwardness of the situation. Khalid knocked on our front door and having delivered me safely left as soon as Mother opened, refusing her invitation to come in.

"How was school?" Mother asked as she took my bag.

"Okay," I replied, avoiding her eyes as much as possible.

"Look, I know your Uncle Attiya's instructions seem hard but he's only doing this for your sake. He is worried about you."

"I know."

The conversation ended there as I disappeared into my room. Father's photograph was in one of the books that I didn't take that day; it lay there on the top of my small desk covered by a few other notebooks and pencils. I got it out immediately and kept staring at it. A few days ago I was angry with him for disappearing. Now, that feeling of guilt came back. I felt stupid for avoiding asking Othman about my Father's disappearance, having to find out from Ahmed instead. Suddenly Uncle Attiya's voice filled the house as mother opened the door for him.

"What do we have for lunch?" he asked Mother loudly.

"I made lentil soup, but I could..."

"No, no, lentils are the nails of the knees. They will do nicely. Ah, here is the little man," he smiled as I opened my door. "How was school?"

I didn't reply, ignoring my Mother's pleading look.

"Khalid tells me you have been a good boy. I think you have learned from your mistake. Look, do not be upset with me. I only want the best for you. I want to treat you as my son."

I hated it when he said that. No one in the world was like my father, especially him. After that beating and after learning that he was keeping something from me, something felt different between us.

I sat down next to Mother, who started chatting to Uncle, complaining about the price of things these days and how everything was getting too expensive. Should I just confront them now? Or should I wait until I have found out more from Um Shadi? Without any proof, it would be pointless to try to accuse them. I opted to quietly sip my soup and started to plan my visit to Um Shadi.

5

Omar stopped writing as the Captain of the flight began announcing that they had one hour left to arrive at Cairo International Airport, giving the usual updates of time of arrival and weather forecast. Around him, the plane was full of white middle-class British businessmen and women, holidaymakers and flight attendants who looked exhausted after clearing up the food trays. Everyone was eager to end their five-hour journey. Omar, though, wasn't sure whether he really wanted the same. His confusion was almost noticeable by other passengers. What he was about to write changed his life forever, made him regret the day he decided to go looking for his father, turned him into a vulnerable person for the rest of his life. He stared at the notebook for a long time before finally deciding to pick up his pen again and carry on, hands shaking, scribbling a few words then crossing them over. This episode of his life was etched in his memory like writings on a stone. It was at that moment that he suddenly became an adult at the age of ten years only.

A week after Uncle's visit, I got home after school to find a letter waiting for me. The minute I had closed the door, Mother thrust the letter under my nose and stared at me. Although it was addressed to me, she had already opened it. There was only one line, asking me to go to El-Markaz for questioning on Friday morning. It was signed by Uri Hrabovsky. My heart dropped at the sight of his signature. Mother stood over me, watching me read the letter.

"What have you done now?" She spoke slowly, dangerously.

"Nothing." I looked up to see her as she lowered her glasses to look at me. There was something strange about the way she gazed at me.

"You know what! Sometimes I feel I don't know you. I don't know my own son."

It took everything inside me not to accuse her of the same.

"What do they want?"

"I do not know. Probably nothing."

"It says 'investigation'. It can't have come from nothing. They must want you for something."

"Mother please, you are frightening me."

She hesitated, and then hugged me really hard.

"Don't worry," she whispered in my ear. "Everything will be fine."

At 8am on Friday morning Mother woke me up. She had baked some lovely Manakish pastries filled with thyme, sesame seeds and olive oil. There was a fresh pot of mint tea waiting on the cloth laid in the middle of the TV room for both of us to sit and eat. I ate quickly and had to rush to the toilet as my stomach was in knots. When I came out, I noticed she had gotten ready too. My fear doubled as I realised Mother was coming with me. Finally, she would discover what I had been up to all this time.

To my utter relief, the soldiers would not allow Mother through the main gates.

"He is only ten years old you bastards!" she yelled at the soldier on the main gate.

"I am sorry, but the letter is in his name. He goes in, you go home."

Though he spoke calmly, he made a point of loading his gun.

Mother drew back, then turned around to hug me goodbye.

"I will ask Uncle Attiya to come as soon as possible. We will come and get you," she promised. Inside, I was made to wait at the main reception, which had a lot of soldiers in it, laughing, smoking and cleaning their guns. One of them was imitating how he shot dead someone in the camp, making fun of how his face had smashed to the ground while the others laughed. I put my hands in my jeans pockets and looked down. I didn't want to see the rest of his re-enactment.

Finally, a soldier came and asked me to follow him into the same long corridor as last time. The urge to go to the toilet was getting stronger, but I didn't dare ask to go. However, instead of the dark, damp room, I was led upstairs and into a spacious and well-lit room. It had windows everywhere, but the glass was so thick that I couldn't hear anything from outside. There was a big desk and two armchairs, a beautiful soft rug and an Israeli flag standing in the corner. On the back wall a big portrait of Theodor Herzl, whose picture I had seen many times in history lessons at school. There were two telephones on the desk, lots of notebooks and a name banner in Hebrew. There were three hunting rifles on the other corner of the room. As I continued to inspect everything with my eyes, the door opened and Uri entered. My stomach started to contort.

"Oh, Omar, *ahlan*, welcome. How very kind of you to respond to our letter."

I had nothing to say to that, I was not sure what to say and certainly hadn't expected such a warm welcome and a greeting in broken Arabic.

"Do sit down, please. Have a seat in that armchair over there. Would you like some water?"

"No, thanks."

Would he beat me for my refusal? He took his dark shades off and opened the drawers of his desk, emptying a case from his pockets into one of them before locking it.

"OK. I won't keep you for too long. You see, I wanted to apologise for last time. I had no idea who you were and who your father was. But after you left I made a few inquiries and realised my mistake."

I leaned over the desk with excitement and he reclined back in his chair as far as he could go, until it was touching the wall behind him and balanced on only two legs.

"I have some information you may find interesting. But first, I want to ask you something Omar. What do you think of us?"

"What do you mean?" I replied carefully.

"I mean, do you think we are bad people?"

I was silent for a long time. Of course I thought he and his soldiers were bad people. They shot and arrested and killed people for no reason. They invaded neighbourhoods and destroyed homes. I had seen all of it firsthand. Of course they were bad people. But I couldn't admit that. He would have me dragged outside and shot in the back.

"I am waiting."

"What does it matter what I think?" I asked, trying to stall for time.

"I want to know what you think and not just what you have been told."

"I know that a lot of people think that you are bad."

"But what about you?"

There was no point pretending. No doubt he already knew what I really thought.

"I don't disagree with them."

I expected a slap on the face and a call for the soldiers to come and beat the shit out of me. Instead, Uri considered me calmly.

"Well, they are wrong, and so are you. You see, we have come here to help your people become civilised. To build roads, schools, universities, machines… To become strong and powerful, like Europe. Wouldn't you like to be like them? A free country to do what you liked in? But what did we get instead? Terrorists blowing themselves up in our neighbourhoods. People shooting at us for no reason."

"I am not sure I want to be like Europe, I have never been, I don't know what it looks like," I interrupted him angrily.

"OK, it seems like a rational discussion is beyond you, so let's try a different tactic here. I have the information you need, which I am happy to give to you. But first, I need a favour in exchange. I will tell you where your father is if you find me information about a masked man who is active with the terrorist group. We know he lives on your street but have been unable to find anyone who seems to know any more than that. You find where he is and I will tell you everything I know about your father."

I glared up at him. "You want me to be an informant?"

"No, I want you to help me eradicate those crazy fanatics that disturb the harmony of our people."

"Those fanatics are the ones defending my people from your soldiers."

Uri's eyes flashed dangerously. I had gone too far.

"I could have you arrested for that. You should be more careful in who you choose to support. Next Friday, I will impose a curfew. You will have a piece of paper with the terrorist's name and house number and will leave it on your windowsill when it gets dark."

"But I don't know the person. Or the house."

"Well, you have a week to find out, if you want to know where your father is. It is your choice Omar," he shrugged as he buzzed the button on his desk and immediately a soldier entered. Uri lit a cigarette and strolled over to one of the windows as the soldier dragged me out of the room.

Mother was waiting outside with Uncle Attiya when I was brought back to the street. She ran straight to me and clasped me in her arms while Uncle followed.

"Are you all right boy?"

"I am fine."

"What happened?" Mother asked as she inspected my body looking for bruises.

"Nothing, they gave me a warning for throwing stones at a patrol last week. Someone said I was involved."

"How many times do I need to tell you to stay out of trouble?" Mother groaned as she took my hand and started walking back home. Uncle walked with us in silence, stopping at a falafel shop and buying us some sandwiches. I didn't have much of an appetite but I forced myself to eat. I was scared and I didn't know what to do. I wanted to tell Mother and Uncle what had happened. They would know what to do. They could help. But for some reason a lie seemed easier than the truth, knowing they were keeping something from me too. I couldn't trust anyone.

In the end, I did not even tell Ahmed about what happened with Uri. I tried to forget about it, cursing myself for going to see Uri in the first place. I would not let him turn me into a spy.

Three days passed and life carried on as usual. On Tuesday of that week, Um Marwan invited me over for a while. She needed help sorting out some of her beautiful embroidery into different sacks. She was highly skilled in making different sketches of beautiful Palestinian embroidery coloured with the green, white, black and red, just like our national flag. She normally sold them to factories to make wall clocks or mirrors and sometimes her patterns were used for dresses and women's clothing. She had promised to make me a jumper with my name on it but never got around to it, as she was always running behind with her work.

I stayed for a long time that day, watching her put the needle into the canvas, carefully creating flowers and other patterns as I sorted her artwork into respective piles. Her husband was outside playing backgammon with other men at the local café by the market. We finished all the work just after midnight, when she got up to prepare some hummus, olives and za'atar for dinner. It was almost 1am when I heard Mother shouting at me from across the street to come back home. I left Um Marwan's house, enjoying the light breeze coming from the sea on such a hot night. The dusty street was in desperate need of some rain.

As I was about to turn the corner, I noticed something move in the distance. I quickly hid behind the electricity pole that stood right in the middle of the street, watching the masked man zigzag from one corner of the street to another, pausing at each as he went. Now I could see that he had a slight limp and despite his vigilance he hadn't noticed me. I kept still as I watched him finally move to the middle of the street and dive into Abu Mohammed's house. Once I was sure I was alone, I ran as fast as I could around the corner and through our front door, which Mother had left open for me. As I leaned against the door to catch my breath, my mind raced. The masked man was not short, fat Abu Mohammed, but he was of similar height to his son.

Zuheir Hammadullah was considered the nicest man in the Jabalia Camp. Everyone loved him for his kindness and relaxed personality. He never got angry with any of the neighbours, unlike his father with his short temper. On rainy days, people in the camp would stack sacks of sand outside their front door to prevent the water from coming in, thus diverting the flood from their house but directing it to another, given how dense the neighbourhood was. Abu Mohammed would go out and shout at his neighbours, ordering them to remove their sacks. His eldest son, Mohammed, would sometimes join him in terrorizing the neighbourhood. But Zuheir would apologise to the neighbours for his father's behaviour.

Zuheir was in his early twenties and was the only one in the street with ginger hair, earning him the rather unimaginative nickname "the Ginger boy". When we played football in the street he would sometimes join my team. The other kids would tease him and tell him to avoid the sun but he would simply laugh and accept the role of goalkeeper, as he was the oldest. He enjoyed playing football with the kids on the street.

He got married last year to a girl from Khan Younis, where Mother came from. The night before the wedding, a massive stag party was thrown for him in the street with a band and a singer. Over four hundred people attended the party, making our narrow street very crowded. Somehow everyone managed to fit, even though there were about fifty chairs that had to be brought out for the elders in his family. It was the first time that a stag party on the street had a belly dancer and a professional Dabke dance troupe with both men and women dancing. A year later, his wife was four months pregnant with their first child.

Zuheir used to work as a mechanic in Gaza City, fixing old cars. His blue uniform was always stained with engine oil, but his long ginger hair always remained tidy and clean. He often limped a bit when he walked due to a toolbox falling on his leg and breaking his ankle. Could that man really be Zuheir? Lying on my bed, I tried to imagine kind, gentle Zuheir as an active member of a resistance group. It didn't seem right. I wish I had not gone to Um Marwan's earlier that day. Recognising him had brought me even more trouble.

I was so nervous the following Friday that it gave me a bad stomach. Mother noticed how many times I ran off to the bathroom and wanted to call for a doctor. I was too busy worrying and feeling miserable to take notice of her. Would the curfew be announced? Perhaps Uri would forget? By late afternoon I was sweating heavily and could do nothing but lie in bed. Mother brought me some camomile to drink every now and again, followed by a cold compress.

And then it was announced: "The curfew would be in place from 6pm until 8am the following morning." Every single part of my body started to shake violently and at some point I found myself crying on my pillow profusely. The entire mission of finding Father could end right there, with a piece of paper left on the windowsill. My life would change again if at least I knew what had happened. I would become a different boy altogether. But in order to do that I had to decide which person to betray, my father or Zuheir, for whom I had so much love and respect. By 8pm, more sweat and frequent trips to the toilet – 9pm silence wraps up the entire neighbourhood; 9:30pm power cut; 10pm Mother goes to bed; 10:30pm one more trip to the toilet after lighting a candle; 10:45pm name left on a piece of paper outside; 11pm sound of boots walking down our street and a hand searching my windowsill; 11:30pm I fall asleep in a pool of sweat.

I was woken up two hours later by a strange, loud noise I didn't recognise. Before I could even try to figure out what was happening, Mother flung my bedroom door open and burst in. She lifted me up in the air in my cover and took me back to her room and ordered me to stay put as she rushed off to see what was happening in the street. I could hear sirens. Vehicles were driving up and down the street at full speed. There were soldiers talking on their walkie-talkies in Hebrew. A faint female voice in the distance saying, "*khalas*, enough, he is not here."

The strange noise became louder. I got up to look outside the window and was blinded by a flashlight. Then gunfire started. I threw myself on Mother's mattress and curled into a ball. Mother returned and lay next to me, hugging me tight.

"Mama, what is that noise?"

"It's a helicopter. They are attacking Abu Mohammed's house. Don't be scared. I am here."

I had already started crying and she did her best to comfort me, but I could not stop. I wanted to tell Mother everything. To confess what I had done in the comfort of her arms and promise her I would abandon my mission once and for all. Instead, I continued crying like a baby falling asleep in his mother's arms.

The curfew was extended until mid-day, so no one was allowed to leave their homes for school or work. I did not want to get out of bed, but Mother came and forced me to shower, which meant filling a big bucket with hot water from the stove. It actually felt good to pour the warm water over my shivering body. I cleaned the last of my tears from my face, but was unable to wash off the feel of guilt that seemed to clog my skin. I had just finished when Mother discovered the electricity was back and rushed to turn the radio on to listen to the news. There was a panel discussion on the *Sawt El-Arab* radio discussing why so many young men were increasingly leaving the Fatah party and joining Hamas. She switched the radio off with a big sigh. It was only when I heard people outside the house that I realised the curfew had been lifted. I went out and saw Um Marwan standing in her normal spot outside her house. Taking my hand, we joined the others as we walked down the already packed street to Abu Mohammed's house. The front door had been blown off. Windows smashed, asbestos sheets broken, it looked like a battle had taken place. Abu Mohammed was showing them around the destruction, his wife and his eldest son, Mohammed, nowhere to be seen.

As we stood there, an open pickup truck came slowly along the crowded street, followed by even more people. I clutched Um Marwan's hand as it passed us. The truck was carrying two bodies, both wrapped in a big Palestinian flag. I caught sight of a flash of ginger hair before Um Marwan pulled me hard towards her, pressed my face into her stomach to prevent me from seeing the dead bodies. Some people started shouting patriotic slogans, others yelled, "*Allahu Akbar*, God is Great, we will revenge our martyr and we will free his brother from prison." I huddled as close to Um Marwan as I could, unable to say a thing.

The funeral procession started to head to El-Shuhada Cemetery, where all martyrs were buried. Um Marwan and I followed as they passed us, but when we reached my house, Um Marwan handed me back to Mother and then carried on with the procession. I watched them leave, staring at their backs. What would they do if they knew the person responsible for all this was standing there behind them? Did they suspect that there was an informant amongst them who gave the information to the enemy? I could still hear their demands for revenge. I saw Abu Mohammed leaning on one of his neighbour's shoulders as he passed me. There was no anger in his face now. Grief had finally taken over. The loss of his son had broken him.

I spent a whole week in bed, refusing to go to school and eating very little. My stress and anxiety tied my stomach in knots and I became very ill. Mother took me to the doctor, who prescribed painkillers. I took some at first to keep her happy but then began throwing them away when she wasn't watching. Ahmed came to visit me several times, bringing his notes from class and helping me with homework. Every day he stayed with me for a few hours after school, before heading home. I did not dare tell him what I had done. Uncle Attiya was unwittingly close when he suggested my illness was caused by the emotional trauma of seeing Zuheir and his mother. I desperately wished I could forget everything.

My depression continued for another six months, my body weak and fragile as I still could not bring myself to eat unless forced. Most of my classmates started bullying me, usually by forcing me out of the queues for water taps or in the canteen. Ahmed became my self-appointed nurse. He would get me food and water when I was at school, though this was actually seldom, as I had taken to skipping classes. Sometimes teachers would send me home halfway through the day when I broke into tears in class, mostly because Mr. Khalil El-Shimali, our geography teacher, would often convince them to. He would come and ask me how I was whenever he saw me. He walked uneasily on crutches, and some of the kids said he was shot by soldiers during one of the demonstrations and his right ankle had been shattered. He always shaved his head and beard, making him look like a soldier. I often looked to see if I could catch a glimpse of a small tattoo of Palestine he had on his left arm.

Mr. Khalil would sometimes take me out of the classroom and put me in a taxi home, asking me to say "hello" to Mother for him. On one occasion, although I was very upset and cried in the middle of our Arabic class, he came from nowhere and asked me to come with him. I didn't want to leave, knowing that Mother would give me a hard time for leaving school again. After resisting for a bit, he lifted me under my shoulders and dragged me out.

"I am doing this for you own good," he told me, dragging me to the street until we found a taxi and he put me in it.

After those terrible six months, I began to feel better but didn't dare go to El-Markaz again to claim my reward.

Ahmed came to visit me one Friday afternoon after prayer and had lunch with us. It was a warm day in May and I was feeling much better, so when Ahmed asked Mother if we could walk along to the beach, she agreed. We were ten-year-old boys whose innocence had been stripped away by so much destruction. We kept to the shaded side of the street, not to avoid the sun but to try and go unseen as much as possible. It felt like the world around us was getting even more dangerous.

We discussed this as we continued to walk up the hilly Twam Road that led to the Jabalia beach, enjoying the light breeze and the faint smell of the sun baking the leaves of the palm trees, even though they were still not in season.

"I am going to Al-Nusairat with my father for a month," Ahmed suddenly announced. "He is running a summer camp once the schools are closed."

I glanced at him, slightly surprised. Abu Ahmed was a PE teacher working for a UN School and he often got paid extra to run summer camps by the beach somewhere in Gaza Strip. He had asked both Ahmed and myself to come with him repeatedly, but we always refused, preferring to escape any regime on our holidays.

"How come you are going?" I asked.

"Well, Dad asked and I thought, why not? It will give me an opportunity to see Um Shadi and question her, if you want me to."

The mention of our old neighbour shook me. With all that had been happening, I had almost forgotten about her. I looked at my friend and smiled, I was so happy to hear that he was still interested in the search.

"Yes. Find out what you can, please," I said, as we continued our walk to the beach.

The water was too cold to swim but we took our shoes off, rolled up our trousers and splashed some water at each other, enjoying a rare moment of calm. A street vendor walked in with his donkey and unleashed it from its heavy cartload on the beach. A couple of heavily armed soldiers walked by. Ahmed turned around as they passed and gave them the middle finger. We laughed and the donkey started braying as if enjoying Ahmed's brave act. His owner was a short fat man, who looked vicious and hardly smiled back at us as we continued to play.

The night before Ahmed was leaving for Al-Nusairat, I went to see him.

"Maybe you can come on the next one, Omar. I am sure Ahmed will love it and will convince you to join. There is one coming up in August."

I nodded politely to Abu Ahmed, though I wasn't betting on it. In the blistering August heat I would fry like an aubergine.

It was dark before I had had the time to say my goodbyes and begin my walk home down the empty streets. Walking through the small alleys, my mind was on Um Shadi and I wondered what Ahmed would bring back. Could there be a different version to how Father disappeared, or had nosy Um Shadi simply got her facts wrong?

Suddenly, I had the uneasy feeling of being watched. I sensed something moving behind me before I got to El-Hawaja Street but every time I turned around the street was empty. The next corner I turned, I ran as fast as I could and hid behind the corner of a nearby house and waited, watching carefully. Finally, a masked man appeared.

Unable to see me and no doubt unaware I was onto him, he started running. I got out of my hiding place and followed him, shouting at him to stop. I managed to follow him several streets until I turned the corner into the Trans Street. There were a few men sitting outside their houses smoking shisha and others walking by. Someone looked at me, startled by my sudden arrival. There was no masked man anywhere. I was catching my breath when an Israeli military jeep put its siren on, piercing my ears. Two soldiers jumped out, one pointing his M16 rifle to my head, so close that I felt it touching my forehead. The other soldier searched me and then clipped his handcuffs to my hand. They shoved me into the car and started driving quickly as they spoke on their radio in Hebrew.

I was not surprised when the jeep approached the walls of El-Markaz. My right leg started to shake so badly that the soldier sitting next to me pressed his arm on it to stop me from doing so. Once we were inside the main gates, the soldiers got out and led me up the now familiar stairs and into Uri's office. He was sitting there with his sunglasses still on the top of his head.

"Ah, there you are! Thanks for dropping by," he said as he ordered the soldier to remove my handcuffs.

"I can't say the pleasure is mutual."

"You know what I like about you Omar," he said quickly, "you have some sense of humour. Unlike the rest of your miserable people."

"Why am I here?"

"Well, I thought you would come back for your information eventually. Wondered what was keeping you, so I decided to send for you. Do you not want to know about your Father?"

I was silent, refusing to dignify him with an answer.

He paused for a bit, looked at some papers and started to sign some documents. Then he let his pen drop on the open book in front of him, took his sunglasses off and glared at me.

"You do, or you don't. Do not waste my time," he said sharply.

"Of course I do!"

"Then you have to do us one last favour."

On hearing these words, I felt the blood freeze in my veins.

"You promised to give me information about Father if I told you the name of the resistance man in our street and I did. You have to honour your word now."

"Oh, I will, but as I said we just want another small favour. Your assistance last time helped the State enormously and you should be proud of yourself."

"No, I won't do this again."

"Yes, you will."

"No I made a terrible mistake and caused the death of innocent people. What about Zuheir's mother? Why was she killed?"

"She got in our way. Sometimes you have to do what is necessary for the greater good."

"I can't see any good in what you are doing," I said sharply. "In fact, I don't want the information about my father any more. You are never going to tell me and I doubt you know anything."

"Listen, you are one of us. You gave us information. We can simply tip off these terrorists about you and they will take care of it. What do you think they will do to you? My guess is they will take a big sharp knife, stick it in your neck and hack their way through you. You will be slaughtered like a worthless chicken. But we are here to protect you now. We are your friends."

"No!" I shouted at him.

He got up and walked quickly towards me. He pushed me against the wall, pinning my arms behind my back easily with one hand, my face pushed against the rough wall. I shouted louder but my voice dried up when he pulled my tracksuit bottoms down, leaving me exposed. In shock, I stopped screaming. I froze, more terrified of Uri than I ever had been.

He ran his hand down my back and grabbed my right butt cheek.

"Look here, idiot, I can do anything I want. I can make you beg for death."

He continued running his hand across my bottom, then through my legs and squeezed my balls. Then he removed his hand and quickly put his middle finger up my butthole. I screamed with pain and started crying, begging him to stop.

"Please, no."

He pushed his finger in and out violently, before taking his trousers off. Blood froze in my veins as I heard the sound of his heavy army belt falling to the ground. Without any delay he pushed his phallus into my tiny body.

"I beg you, no, please...please."

I begged for what felt like hours before he finally stopped and went to the sink in the corner to wash up. I pulled my trousers up quickly as I sobbed, my stomach gurgling like a boiling kettle.

"You will do as I say," he said as he continued to wash his hands.

"Yes." I hardly recognised my voice.

"Yes, Sir," he shouted back at me.

"Yes, Sir."

"Someone will tell you what we need you to do. Get out now."

I slowly walked home with my head down, staring at the dusty street while I tried to ignore the pain. I needed to go to the toilet urgently and thought about knocking on someone's door and asking for permission to use their facilities, but did not want to make a scene so I continued home. Mother was still in the living room, sewing an old pair of jeans of mine. She didn't say anything when I opened the door, as she knew I had been with Ahmed and it was only 10pm. But she let out a scream when she saw me in the light.

"Is that blood on your foot? What happened to your foot?" She bent down to inspect my trousers but I stopped her quickly.

"Oh, nothing, it's just a scab that I scratched. I will wash it off in the shower."

I hurried to the bathroom. I hadn't realised I was still bleeding. The blood was everywhere down my thighs and legs. It was a frightening sight but worse still was that both my underpants and trousers were full of blood. Mother would undoubtedly find out when she washed them. How would I explain what happened? I could hear her pacing up and down our small corridor. I wanted to hide in the bathroom forever. The best option was to wash them myself and then think about what to tell her.

Scrubbing those tracksuit bottoms was satisfying. I was angry and scared and confused. I wanted to shower for days, then find an Israeli jeep and start throwing stones at it until they shot me and everything would be finished. I thought of Father and what he would think of what happened today, of his worthless coward son who was now an informant to the army that had stolen our land and tortured our people for decades. Would he comfort his son? Or would he disown me?

It was all my fault, I should have told Uri yes from the beginning. After today, I felt there was no reason for me to stay alive anymore. The only other option I felt that I had was to grab a knife from the kitchen and stick it into my heart.

When I finished in the shower, Mother was still waiting for me outside. She wrapped me in a towel and carried me to my room. She dressed me in fresh pyjamas and put me in bed, telling me a story from my favourite book, *Kalila wa Dimna*.

"Once upon a time," she began in her soft voice, gently stroking my hair, "there was a lion that was loved by all the animals in the jungle. His particular companion was a lazy hyena who stayed with him all the time and ate all the mighty lion's leftovers. But one day, the lion became very ill, so he could hardly move or hunt, while his companion went hungry as there were no leftovers anymore. The lion told the hyena that his illness could only be cured if he ate the heart and ears of a donkey. Pretending to be faithful, his companion promised to bring a donkey for the lion and went off in search of one. He eventually found one working hard in a field that it was ploughing every day for its farmer.

"The hyena told the donkey he should not obey his master, and that it should run off instead to a place where a herd of donkeys lived happily in the jungle. The donkey got excited and ran off immediately, the hyena running ahead to inform the lion that the donkey was on his way. The lion started roaring from a distance and before he jumped out of the bushes the donkey got scared and ran off before seeing the lion. Embarrassed, the lion explained that his illness had made him slow and that should he see the donkey again he would surely jump on it and rip his chest open to get the heart. The hyena chased the donkey again and asked him why he ran off so quickly. The donkey explained that he was frightened of the lion's roar, but the hyena explained that the sound was not a lion's, rather the noise of the collective herd of donkeys coming all together to welcome him in their territory."

"The donkey fell for the lie and went back with the hyena. This time the lion was ready and as soon as they approached, he jumped on the donkey with all his might and killed him with one hit of his claws. He then ripped his heart open but said to the hyena that he had to wash before he ate them, as the doctors advised. When he left, the hyena quickly ate the donkey's heart and ears. When the lion returned, he was surprised to not find his prescription. He asked the hyena who said that if the donkey had a heart and ears it wouldn't have come back."

6

At Cairo Airport, Omar was nervous as he held his British passport tightly in the queue. He knew there would be a lot of questions from the middle-aged officer with the dark thick moustache sitting behind the immigration desk. He had done this journey before and it always amused him being asked the same questions every time. But somehow he felt that this time it was going to be harder than ever.

"Where are you from?" the officer asked as he got to the immigration desk.

"I am sorry, did I not give you my passport?"

"Don't be a smart-arse, I know you have a British passport but I asked you where you are originally from."

"Palestine."

"Why are you not speaking Arabic then? Where's your Palestinian passport?" Omar grabbed his other document and handed it to him.

"What are you waiting here for? Go and wait over there and we will call out your name soon."

Omar knew that the wait would take a long time, but was still disappointed that his British passport would not save him from the torturous bathroom-sized deportation room, where he would be waiting to be put on a bus destined for the Rafah Border Crossing and then squeezed into the Gaza Strip like all other Palestinians.

As he sat down watching endless queues of Egyptians, Europeans and other nationalities going through immigration, he got out his phone to text Zoe and tell her that he had arrived in Cairo. He also scrolled down Twitter and news pages again, but there was no more news of his house yet, no names, just images of rubble. He took out his notebook again.

A month later, Ahmed returned from his summer camp and immediately came to see me. Mother prepared some snacks for us while he told me all about the camp and the new survival skills he acquired, boasting in particular about his ability to make fire with two stones, which I was very interested to see. He hadn't expected to enjoy the time away as much as he did and, to his surprise, he found his father rather easy-going. Ahmed would often burst into one of the new patriotic songs he had learnt. He sang about the homeland and how we should fight for our right to be in the land of our grandfathers, never submitting to the new colonial rule of the Israelis. The songs made me feel ashamed of myself, and I would lower my gaze to the floor as he proudly raised his voice and clapped his hands. Eventually Mother left to go visit my uncle, and Ahmed waited until the door was completely closed before jumping to his story.

"Listen, I've got something to tell you," he said the moment we saw Mother leaving the house, shutting the door behind her. "I saw Um Shadi in the small market in Al-Nusairat. She says hello and asked after you and your mother."

I was silent. I wanted him to tell the story and be done with it. A big part of me regretted the whole thing.

"It took a lot of convincing to get her to tell me what she knew about your father's disappearance. She asked why I was interested and said that it was not any of my business. I said that you wanted to know but she was having none of it. Then I said Othman had already told us anyway and that you would tell your Mother about what she had told Othman. She cringed when she heard that and I knew it had worked. She couldn't afford a big fight with a formidable woman like your mother."

I smiled because Ahmed was clearly pleased with himself for his quick thinking. He had that one chance of questioning her and he was determined to get all the answers he wanted.

"She told me that on the night that your father disappeared, she heard loud noises coming out of the house. She looked out of the window and saw no one in the street but recognised your father's voice. He was shouting something like 'No, I won't give up, it is my right'. Your uncle was shouting back at him saying, 'It's too late, you fool, it's been decided – we are certain'. Then Um Shadi heard something like glass breaking and your mother crying. When Um Shadi heard that, she looked out of the window again and saw your father leave and slam the door behind him. There was nothing for a few minutes, then your uncle left the house quietly. And that's it."

"So, the same version as Othman told us?" I asked looking, unimpressed by his revelations.

"We need to find out what the argument was about."

"Right, and how do you suppose we do that?"

He didn't appreciate the sarcasm in my voice after all his hard work.

"Listen, Um Shadi mentioned there was a dispute about the house. Apparently, your father was never happy with the share he had. She said that everyone on the street was shocked when the house was divided between your father and your uncle and how disproportionate the shares were. I think that's good enough a thread to follow, don't you think?"

"I always assumed that Uncle had a bigger house because he had a big family," I replied shortly. My mind was busy comparing Mother and Um Shadi's versions again. "Why do you think Uncle called Father a fool?"

"I have no idea," Ahmed shrugged, "but it sounds like your father and your uncle had a massive argument about the house. I would keep an eye on your uncle if I were you."

"But why wouldn't Mother tell me of all that? Why hide it?"

"I don't know, my friend. Perhaps she is frightened?"

I sadly closed the door after Ahmed left, hating being left alone in that cursed house. Loneliness suffocated me as I paced up and down the corridor, thinking about Father. Mother's version was starting to make less and less sense. Why would someone disappear just like that, unless there was some dispute that pushed him over the edge? Was Uncle trying to get rid of him to take over the house? What was Mother frightened off? Then I remembered how vicious Uncle could be, like that day he had beaten me with his belt. Had he really meant to hurt me? Perhaps Ahmed was right; perhaps I should be keeping an eye on Uncle. Maybe I should be looking for more proof to confront him with. There might have been something useful hidden in Uncle's house.

I had to wait several months before daring to do anything. I had decided to wait until September 1991, when schools started again and the house would more likely to be empty. Meanwhile, I kept watch on the house and paid more attention to Uncle's and his family's routine. He left the house every day at 5am in the morning and came back at 8pm. My cousins left for school at 8am and came back at 4pm. His wife went to the market to do the shopping at 9am and stayed there for a couple of hours before she came back laden with shopping bags of fresh vegetables. That would be my best opportunity to search without being caught.

Not long after school had started, I heard Mother and Uncle's wife agreeing one morning to go to the market the next day together. It was perfect; with Mother for company, she would be even longer at market than usual.

The next morning, I pretended to leave for school but instead wandered through the alleyways trying to avoid people as I waited for Mother to leave. When I got back, Um Marwan was just about to start her day, sitting in the same spot. She was startled to see me and asked if I was okay. I waved and explained I had left one of my books at Uncle's house that I needed for that day's classes. Instead, I fetched Uncle's spare key and headed to his house. Once I let myself in, I figured the best place to start searching would be Uncle's room. It was extremely neat, with a tidily made bed with pristine sheets and a brown old oak wardrobe and chest of drawers that had barely a speck of dust on them. There were pictures of Grandfather and Grandmother hung on the wall and a picture of him in his youth on the beach in Haifa.

The whole room smelled of strong aftershave, which made me sneeze a couple of times. It was some sort of cheap make that Uncle used every day before going to work.

I figured I had about an hour and a half before Uncle's wife would be home, so I idly began to search the wardrobe, not really knowing what to look for. There was jewellery, a make-up kit, a leather case with shaving materials in it, an old watch lying on one of the shelves and a few books here and there and the piles of clothes mixed together without separating them into Uncle's and his wife's sections. I marvelled at the contrast between how neat the room was and how messy the wardrobe.

I looked under the bed, above the wardrobe, in the chest of drawers, but could find nothing of interest, let alone importance. After another search of the wardrobe I eventually lost patience and slammed one of the doors shut. To my frustration, one of the books fell out. I cursed and bent to pick it up, then noticed a piece of paper that had fallen out of the pages it had been tucked into. I stooped to reach it, praying it was not a bookmark, since I had no idea where it had been. But it wasn't a bookmark. It was a letter addressed to Uncle:

16 April 1981

Dear Mr. Attiya,

Assalamu Aleikum.

We refer to your earlier correspondence with regards to your brother Mr. Mustafa Ouda's property. We would like to inform you that our records indicate that Mr. Mustafa has already registered his right as owner of number 182/6 Sanaida Street. We understand your current concerns but unfortunately we must wait for further instruction from Mr. Mustafa Ouda with regards to the changes. Any enquiries related to this dispute should be directed to us only.

Yours sincerely,

Khayyam El-Farra
Barakat Solicitors
El-Wihda Street
Gaza City

I put the letter back in its place, my mind buzzing. So, Uncle had been enquiring about the house. I wanted to speak to Ahmed immediately and tell him what I had found out. Satisfied with my success, I returned the book to the wardrobe and decided to leave before I managed to get myself in any more trouble. I put the letter back in its place, my mind in great confusion.

Since Ahmed would still be at school, I decided to go for a walk, heading out of Jabalia and along to the beach. I stopped when I saw the waves and sat on the hot sand. I spent the rest of the afternoon there, before leaving to catch Ahmed on his route home to avoid being caught by any teachers. I caught up with him in a small alley just before Hawaja Street.

He was surprised to see me there in my school uniform and my bag. I explained everything to him and described what I had found out. There was a big smile on his face, happy I had taken his suspicions seriously. He begged me to let him go to the law firm to make some enquiries, as it had been his idea to investigate my uncle.

The following Monday, he met me in the courtyard with a look of disappointment on his face. He said he had been told that the firm closed down some years ago and the owner had moved to Egypt with his family. There was no trace of anyone called Khayyam El-Farra. No one seemed to remember him or the name. Someone said the name rang a bell but couldn't really give any more details. Another said he was just a trainee solicitor who stayed with the firm for a few months before being arrested by the Israeli army on charges of belonging to the Fatah resistance group. Just as we thought we were making a breakthrough with our investigations, things ground to a halt again. There was no way either of us could go to Egypt to investigate.

I received Uri's orders in October. During one geography class, Mr. Khalil approached my desk and asked to see my notebook. As I moved it for him to inspect, he dropped a folded piece of paper into it and moved on. Frowning, I opened it and found a small note scribbled on it:

"Find out the mystery of Block 8 as you did in your Block 6."

My heart dropped as I glanced at Mr. Khalil realising immediately he must know what I had done. Even more disturbing was that he was a collaborator just like me. How else would he have known to pass on the message? I stared at him for a long time as he continued with his class.

I was scared and felt sick. I had thought that the Israelis forgot about me, deciding that I was actually of no use to them. But clearly they had been waiting for the right moment. Now I had to play spy again, or they would make sure my head is chopped off by the resistance movement.

I excused myself from class and ran to the bathroom just as the vomit filled my mouth. When I came back, shaking and pale, Mr. Khalil sent me home just as he had done many times before. No one suspected anything.

Two days later, I came back to class with a small note in my geography notebook and handed it to Mr. Khalil. I had spent the last two days watching the street and wrote the date, time and house number that the masked man came out of. That same evening there was a curfew and no electricity and eventually gunshots could be heard in the distance. The next morning, members of the Hamas resistance group announced from the speakers in their small pickup that one of their leaders had been arrested along with two members of the party. My stomach lurched as they passed, but I kept my head down and continued on my way.

As the months passed, I was forced to pass this sort of information to Mr. Khalil again and again. I had unwillingly become an experienced informant, and every time I handed over the information, I wished the earth would open up and swallow me completely.

I was in too deep. No one would understand how all I had wanted was information about my father. They would not care how Uri had bullied me into doing such an awful act. I avoided thinking about Father to keep even more shame from coming my way. Surely he would be disgusted to know what I was doing. It helped that there was a demonstration almost every day in the camp and our school was always the first to join in. Soldiers were often there too, searching for what they claimed to be “hiding” resistance fighters. They never found anyone, but continued their search until their inspections became so intense and frequent that it caused considerable disruption to our studies. It took me a while to realise that this must be how they passed their orders to Mr. Khalil, who would in turn act on them or pass on my own orders. The headmaster suspended lessons every time the soldiers came, asking us to go out in the yard while they searched.

In 1992, we were given our fifth grade awards. I was eleven -and-a-half years old and didn't know how I had managed to pass to the next year; we had only managed four full days at school that year, no one had studied and there had been no exams again. I still made sure to take part in the demonstrations by throwing stones at Israeli soldiers. It was not fuelled by my patriotism, but my anger against the soldiers whom I had seen arrest, kick, attack and beat people in front of my eyes, sometimes as a result of my own actions.

7

"Where's the exit stamp on your Palestinian passport?" the hairy Egyptian officer was shouting at Omar.

"I don't have one, we don't need one when we leave the UK, especially now that I travelled on my British passport." Omar was surprised by the question.

"Ah well, things have changed here I am afraid, we can't send you to Gaza without an exit stamp from the country you came from."

"So what do I do then?"

"You can either return back and get a stamp, or take another flight to another country, use your British passport, then leave with your Palestinian one." Omar was shocked to hear this, he didn't know what to do. The thought of going back to Heathrow and wasting all this time and money was making him sick. He needed to get to Gaza, he needed to search for everyone.

"You need to let me know what you want to do so we can put you on the next flight." The officer was impatient.

"Can I take a flight to Jordan?"

"If there's one available, go and wait there, someone else will come and take you to the airlines desk to see what's available."

I was twelve-and-a-half years old when I was shot for the first time, and far worse than the pain in my leg was the fact that no one was allowed to visit me in hospital for the first three days, as ordered by the Israeli officer in charge of the hospital.

It had been a warm day in spring. The sky was clear, and almond trees were beginning to blossom, a sign that the earth was waking up, yawning and stretching after months of silent sleep. I had left home early to go to school, not really paying attention to my mother's daily instructions about traffic, doing well, not falling asleep in the classroom, and, most importantly, not throwing stones at Israeli tanks. Thousands of mothers all over Gaza gave similar instructions to their children every day, only in my case it usually went in one ear and out the other. Throwing stones had become a great sport that I wasn't going to give up easily. It had become the highlight of my day and the main driver for going to school. It made me release all the anger I had for those bastards who abused me.

On that particular day I had somehow managed to keep all the promises I had made, so on the way home in the early afternoon I was feeling particularly proud and virtuous. I was casually kicking a football around with three of my friends as we walked. We joked, talked about girls, kicked dust at each other, until we rounded the last corner and realised we had just walked into hell.

Five Israeli military jeeps packed with soldiers had stopped, forming an island of metal in the middle of the uneven, rocky road. Then they opened fire. No warning. Just a hail of bullets everywhere. People were running, others were throwing stones, and some could only stand and scream with fear and desperation. The gentleness of the day was shattered by the gunfire, the whine of the bullets, and the shrieking of women. For one split second, the three of us did nothing. We simply stood and watched the death and devastation unfolding in front of us like it was some kind of a movie. But we couldn't stay out of it for long, and as if we were one person instead of three, my friends and I hurled down our schoolbags and picked up something to throw.

My mother's instructions to stay out of trouble were forgotten and I was back playing my favourite game. We threw stones and dodged the snarling bullets coming from the direction of the soldiers. We hid behind the blocks of broken concrete and the rubble and rubbish that littered the street and continued to throw more rocks. I found myself trapped in a corner of the square. In front of me a soldier knelt in the dust, pointed his rifle at me and took aim. I started to shake. I remembered the masked man who fired in the air. I remembered the sound of bullet ripping through the air and how terrifying it sounded.

I didn't know what to do so I smiled. I started unloading the stones I was carrying, and kept on smiling. I realised that the soldier wasn't smiling back. He just continued to kneel in the dirt with his gun pointing at me, his face devoid of any emotion. I felt the fear growing from the bottom of my feet up to my head, creeping upwards like a malignant vine until I was completely covered. The day grew suddenly cold. He was still kneeling and pointing his gun directly at me. He pulled the trigger, and his rifle spat flame.

The sound of his gun tore through the air, and I suddenly felt as if my leg had been caught in a saw. The pain was indescribable, like a great black, swooping bird of agony that swept down and grabbed me with its talons and threw me to the ground. Everything that was happening around me suddenly seemed far away. Even the pain in my leg and my ears seemed remote. I closed my eyes, thinking about how cross Mother would be because my new school trousers were stained with blood and full of holes. She'd kill me when she found out. I could smell smoke in the air, tyres burning, heat, blood, fear. I couldn't breathe. I was drowning. Nothing was real. I was so tired.

Blackness.

When I opened my eyes, Uri was standing there in the middle of my room. I let out a big cry of pain the moment my eyes spotted him. He was looking at me with disdain.

"What are you playing at?" he shouted at me the moment he saw my eyes open. I did not respond. "Well, suit yourself, don't talk. But next time I am going to order the soldiers to shoot you dead."

"I want to see my mother. Where is she?"

"No one is coming to see you unless I say so."

"I did not ask to be shot. I did not beg your stupid soldier to shoot me."

"Then you should stay out of these things. Your job is to report the ones who throw the stones and cause trouble, not throw the bricks yourself. Don't fuck with us, Omar. You know what we are capable of doing." He slammed the door behind him.

The hospital stank of cleaning products and old medicine. Every time a nurse opened the door, I could see a soldier standing outside. He would search the nurse before she came in and then keep a close eye on everything she did. She never said a word to me, focusing on treating my wound and asking how I was. I was sure that she knew everything about my collaboration with the soldiers. She was one of the most beautiful women I had ever seen, with striking black eyes framed by thick eyelashes. She would flash her white teeth on the rare occasion that she smiled while I whined about the smell of the hospital or the quality of the food.

The first person to visit me was not my mother but Mr. Khalil. I was asleep when he entered, but when he sat on my bed I woke up. Seeing him there, a familiar face, a comrade in the same terrible position I had found myself in, I finally broke down.

"Mr. Khalil, please. I can't do this anymore."

He didn't say a word, but just touched my bandages and looked at me wide-eyed.

"Please," I begged, "tell them to go away. I can't do it anymore. I really can't." He continued to look at me for a few moments. Then he told me everything.

Mr. Khalil told me that he was an active member of a local resistance group that belonged to Fatah. He loved Palestine and the national cause, and threw stones and fired guns at Israeli soldiers on numerous occasions. In the seventies, aged twenty, he was one of the key people who helped kidnap a soldier and bargained with Israel for the release of many Palestinian prisoners. They in turn knew who he was and tried on several occasions to assassinate him, without success.

Mr. Khalil's wife died while giving birth to their son, Izzat, who was born with a heart problem that meant it was too weak to pump blood to the rest of his body. He needed an operation in Tel Aviv, as the main El-Shifa Hospital in Gaza City did not have the equipment or expertise to perform such a complex operation on him. After months of endless paperwork and bureaucracy from the Israeli army, a permit was issued for both of them to go to the Erez Crossing between the Gaza Strip and Israel, where an Israeli ambulance was waiting on the other side of the crossing. When Khalil got there, his new-born baby wrapped up in his arms, he was immediately arrested and taken for questioning. The son was placed in the ambulance and attended to by three doctors from Meir Hospital in Kfar Saba, Tel Aviv.

Khalil was questioned by the Israelis about his participation in the resistance movement, but denied the allegations completely. The officer in charge of the questioning then put a gun to his head and said that if he did not collaborate, he would shoot him on the spot. When Khalil refused to admit to anything, another officer in the room came forward and said that if he did not give the names of other resistance fighters, his son's papers would be cancelled and he would not be able to receive treatment.

I watched Mr. Khalil, understanding that his choice had been even harder than mine. He had to either betray his country or his child. If he took his son back to Gaza, he would not survive. The Israelis knew that he was an active member of the resistance movement and could have put him in jail on an administration sentence, meaning that he would not face court or be sentenced and could stay there for the rest of his life. But he was too important with a lot of valuable information, and knowing he would not confess easily, they would have to bargain with him.

He kept staring at the top left corner of the room, where the cracked wall met the ceiling. There was a large spider crawling slowly as he continued to tell me how things moved on.

A month later, most of his comrades were either arrested or killed. The operation in Israel could not save Izzat and he passed away. And thus Khalil became one of the most important informants within the camp. His peers respected him so much that no one could suspect him, not least because of his long record of patriotism. Like me, he had to carry on informing, even after his son died. There was no way back for him because the Israelis would have informed the resistance that Mr. Khalil was an informant. One of his ex-colleagues who had been arrested wrote to him, asking him to be the guardian parent of his five-year-old daughter, Rihana. Since then, he dedicated his life to looking after her. He never remarried and did not want to have another child. He was satisfied with what he got in the end, though he was haunted by guilt. He broke ranks with the resistance gradually and finally handed Uri his gun in a public show at El-Markaz.

Uri addressed people who were gathered outside, telling them the important step Mr. Khalil had made and how he hoped it would form a precedent for all freedom fighters to follow. People lost respect for Mr. Khalil, accusing him of being a coward. A year later, he obtained his teaching diploma and became a geography teacher in my school. He had a car accident soon after, which left him paralysed for a while, then dependent on crutches. Rihana grew up to be a beautiful girl and she loved him like a father. He worked tirelessly to give her everything she wanted and when it was time for her to go to university, he paid for her to go to the US to study engineering. He continued collaborating with the Israelis. There was no way back for him.

"There's still time, Omar," he smiled as he opened the door and exited. I did not understand what he meant and it gave me little comfort.

I was delighted when Ahmed finally came to visit me; I had not realised my visitor ban had been lifted. He and his father had even brought chocolate and delicious *shawarma* sandwiches with them. The taste of chicken with garlic sauce and salad revived me after spending a whole week eating stale hospital food. They asked me how I felt and whether the injury still hurt but I reassured them the painkillers were working.

"The doctor says I was lucky. No shattered bones, just through the flesh and out the other side. With a bit of luck, I would be on my feet in the next three weeks."

"*Inshallah*," Ahmed's father said while Ahmed grinned.

"Father, can I stay with Omar tonight?" he asked enthusiastically. I was very happy at the thought of company and looked pleadingly at Abu Ahmed.

"If it is all right with the nurses, then of course. But Omar's mother must agree too. She might want to stay herself and this room is too small for three people."

"I don't know if she knows that the visiting ban has been lifted," I said quickly.

"Very well then, I will come and pick you up tomorrow. Don't chat all night. Omar needs to rest. I will have a word with the doctor and then pick up more food for you. I will also pass by your mother's on the way home and let her know the good news."

I watched him as he hugged Ahmed before he left, and wished that he was my father, too.

Ahmed wanted to hear everything about how it had happened. There was a look of admiration in his eyes when I described how I threw stones at the soldiers. In those days, it was considered patriotic to be injured by soldiers. If only he knew the traitor I actually was.

As we sat there chatting, the door suddenly opened and Uncle Attiya burst into the room. Ignoring Ahmed completely, he swooped and kissed me on the cheek and hugged me.

"*Hamdellah ala es-salameh*, thank God for your safety. We were so worried." His voice sounded hoarse.

"Where is Mother?" I said quickly.

"She wanted to come but I told her to wait until the morning. It is late and not very safe for a woman to travel on her own all the way from Jabalia to Gaza City. Look, I brought you some chocolate."

He sat by the bed and asked me about everything that had happened. Unlike Ahmed, he was not very impressed. He stared at me, a dangerous fire burning in his eyes. He asked how the hospital staff were treating me and whether the Israelis had mistreated me. He was confused about my visitor restrictions, why even my own mother was banned from seeing me for a whole week.

"The bastards! How can they deny a mother from seeing her injured son?"

I remained silent. It was obvious to me; I knew that it was Uri punishing me.

"I must be off now, work in the morning. But listen here, young man. I am glad you are fine and that you will recover soon, but trust me, if you ever pick up a stone and throw it at the soldiers again, I will lock you in that house of yours and you will never see daylight again. Do you understand me?"

There was that tone of anger in his voice that frightened me. I looked at Ahmed for some help but he did not respond, instead he looked down and pretended to be exploring the boxes of chocolate Uncle brought.

"I would have stayed to keep an eye on you but for that damned work in Israel I need to wake up early. Besides you've got a good lad here next to you. I am sure you two will have a good night. Try to get some sleep."

As he often did, he slammed the door as he left. Ahmed looked at me apprehensively, not knowing what to say.

"I wish Father was here," I said quietly, ignoring the tear that fell.

Ahmed came closer and put his hand on my shoulder.

"We will find him, I promise."

Mother came in the morning and gave me a hug that knocked the wind out of me, crying like I had never seen her cry before. As she didn't ask what had happened, I assumed she had heard my version from Uncle. She brought lots of food with her, clothes to change in and some of my toys and schoolbooks. If I had ever needed proof that my mother loved me, I saw it in her eyes that day as she stroked my hair and smiled at me. She looked very pretty in her white Palestinian embroidered dress and men in the hospital stopped to look at her when she passed by. The doctor became extra nice to me once he met Mother.

8

I stayed in hospital for one more week, during which Ahmed did not come back to visit me again. I was surprised but supposedly he was busy studying, or perhaps his father felt that one night he had stayed with me was enough. Um Marwan visited me daily and stayed for most of the day, even when Mother was around. She brought her embroidery work with her and sat on a chair in the corner and carried on, sometimes speaking to Mother, asking her whether she had given me the painkillers, were my bandages perhaps a little too tight, what on earth were they feeding me in this place? She even stayed a couple of nights, insisting that Mother should go home to take a rest. Um Marwan held my hand as I limped out of my hospital bed and left the hospital with Uncle and Mother. A seven-seater Mercedes taxi was waiting for us outside and drove us through El-Naser Street, then to the Twam Junction, before descending down the beach road back to the Jabalia Camp.

A hero's welcome was waiting for me in the street. All the neighbours, kids and other unfamiliar faces gathered outside and started clapping as I got out of the taxi. Well-wishers had come from everywhere when they heard I was being discharged from hospital. Mother looked proud as she led me through the parade of happy faces. In the house, there was a feast ready for me that she had prepared before she came to pick me up. Uncle Attiya sat in the middle of the front room to receive visitors, standing up every time someone came in and showing people the door as they prepared to leave. Some kids from my school, many of whom I didn't know very well before, came as well; they peered into my room every now and again and gave me little presents they managed to gather from their personal belongings or that their parents had bought for me. My favourite was Ali's personal ruler, which I had admired many times in class. It had a picture of Jerusalem on it and when he twisted it a Palestinian flag appeared and wrapped around the El-Aqsa Mosque. It was his most precious belonging and I took it with delight.

A feeling of sadness overtook me every time the door shut and I was left alone in the room. I did not deserve the hero's welcome that everyone gave me. If only they knew, they would probably all jump on me in one go and suffocate me to death. Neither Uncle nor Mother would be able to stop them. My bed was the only place where I could hide in and be who I was without anyone being able to judge me. I did not mean to be a collaborator or a hero. I had managed to tangle myself in a horrible situation, but the people around me would not understand.

There was still no sign of Ahmed a week after I had got out of hospital. Mother asked if we had had an argument or if I had said something to upset him. One day, while I was sitting receiving the constant waves of visitors like a king on his throne, Ahmed's father came to see me. He barely touched his mint tea, instead paced awkwardly around the room, almost refusing to mingle with the other guests. Once the rest of the neighbours left and only he and Uncle Attiya remained, he told us Ahmed had been missing for ten days now. They had looked everywhere for him. Abu Ahmed had put off visiting me because he knew I had just come out of hospital and needed to rest, but he could no longer hold off coming to ask if I knew anything.

With a sinking feeling, I watched Abu Ahmed trying to hold

back his tears as he told us they had searched the whole of the camp, Gaza City and as far afield as Khan Younis and Rafah. They had asked all hospitals and mosques. They even asked at El-Markaz with no word from them at all.

"Omar, *habibi*, did he say anything when he stayed with you in hospital? He disappeared three days after," he told me in desperation.

"Nothing. Nothing that would explain why he would disappear like that. We talked about schoolwork, my injury, just normal stuff."

I kept my head down as I answered, unable to look him in the face.

"Very well. If you remember anything, please let me know. You can't move properly right now, but perhaps your uncle can come and inform us."

"Yes, of course," Uncle Attiya replied for me. "I am so sorry to hear this and *Inshallah* you will find him soon. Please let me know if we can help with anything. I will come and check on you soon."

Mother looked at me suspiciously the moment the door was closed. I hadn't noticed that she was staring hard at me. It was another week before I managed to get to school. It was another lovely sunny day in May and it felt good to be out of the house. I wanted to walk to school, even though I was still using my crutches. But Uncle Attiya insisted that he got a taxi for me, despite my constant protests. Um Marwan was in her usual spot and was very happy to see me out in the street.

"*Hamdellah ala es-salameh*, thank God you're safe, Omar," she shouted as I got in the taxi smiling back at her. It felt good to be back in the same old routine. I limped my way between classes and tried hard to avoid meeting eyes with Mr. Khalil when we crossed paths. I wanted the whole thing to be over; he was a constant reminder of the trouble I was in. On my first day, passing him as he leaned against the back wall of the school, I noticed his crutches on the floor. Suddenly it hit me how much we had in common. We were both limping spies.

The story of my getting shot had quickly disappeared from people's minds once they realised Ahmed had vanished. Everyone at school had some explanation or another for it. Some said he had been killed by the Israelis and buried somewhere. Others said that he ran away. But as for me, I knew that Ahmed was alive somewhere and that he would come back if he could, just like my father. On the way home I felt sad and lonely. Now I had two people to look for.

I ignored the taxi that was waiting for me after school that afternoon on Uncle's orders. The driver started beeping at me but I shouted at him to go. I walked slowly until I got near Ahmed's house. There were lots of men sitting outside sipping coffee. I recognised some of them as his uncles. It almost looked like a funeral party. Abu Ahmed was looking tired and had lost a noticeable amount of weight. Perhaps it was all his walking to the police station or the hospitals, checking for any information he could find about his son. It had been three weeks now since Ahmed had disappeared.

Abu Ahmed caught sight of me coming down the street and met me with a hug. The man sitting next to him stood up and went inside the house, leaving the chair for me to sit next to Abu Ahmed. Soumaya, Ahmed's sister, peered out and gave me a smile. My heart broke to see her so sad, her eyes red and puffy from recent tears. I sat down with the other men who were chatting about the prospect of a peace agreement between us and the Israelis that had been reported in the news.

I listened carefully to everything that was said, unsure whom to agree with. One thing I knew for sure was that I wanted all the killings and arrests to stop. I couldn't bear it anymore. Worse still was the fact that I was part of this killing myself, even if it was technically in an indirect way. The thought began to suffocate me as I sat outside with the men, listening to more debates and arguments for and against the Oslo negotiations.

Out of nowhere, Uncle Attiya appeared. The men stood up to greet him by shaking his hand, as was the custom when a new person arrived. Uncle looked tired and was breathing heavily. Abu Ahmed gave him a chair and sat him opposite me. He kept staring at me as he exchanged all the pleasantries with the other men, making me squirm in my seat. He told Abu Ahmed that he was there to check on him and whether there was any news of Ahmed, but he would glare at me every now and again. He was always very pleasant when people asked about Mother or his kids or me in public. He told them about our daily activities, as if we were the most perfect family in the whole of the Gaza Strip. Meanwhile, he stared at me with a mean look.

"Are you coming home with me?" he finally asked.

"Yes. I would like to walk though." I was not asking but more like giving an order publicly which he would not be able to refuse in front of everyone.

"Very well then, let us."

We walked in silence for most of the way. I refused his help and relied on the crutches as much as I could, which meant I had to rest a couple of times. He was obviously very angry with me as he hardly looked me in the eye. Sometimes he walked a few metres ahead of me, so that passers-by wouldn't think that we were family.

But just before we got to the house, Uncle turned around and faced me with a baleful look in his eyes.

"Your father made terrible mistakes. Don't be a fool like him."

He then marched on ahead of me again, ignoring my pleas for him to stop and explain, as if I didn't exist. I continued to shout at his back as I broke into an awkward run with my crutches.

"What do you mean? Tell me!" I shouted.

He had vanished now. In frustration, I threw my crutches on the ground and forced myself to run, ignoring the pain. All I wanted to do at that moment was to catch up with Uncle and beat the answer out of him.

I ran all the way to Uncle's house and banged on the door until a surprised Khalid answered. I demanded to see Uncle but he informed me that his father was not home. I sat at the corner of my house while Um Marwan stared at me without saying a word. She must have seen the tears in my eyes. Eventually, Mother came and found me there. She ordered me inside immediately and I obliged, not wanting to have an argument with her. She was shocked to see me limping without crutches and asked what had happened. I simply said that I felt better and that I would not need them anymore.

I looked at the mirror after washing my face, watching the water drip down my wide forehead. My hair had grown as curly and thick as Father's in the photograph. My lips were thin too, just like his. My skin was fairer though. I found myself looking down at my feet and sizing up my height, wondering whether he was my four-foot-seven height when he was my age, twelve years old. My shoulders were beginning to look as wide as his looked in the photograph. I settled down for dinner with Mother and decided to tell her what Uncle had said. She was livid but claimed she had no idea what he meant.

"Don't worry about what he says. He was always jealous of how popular your father was. I wouldn't be upset, people say things they don't mean sometimes".

"It's about the house, isn't it?" I asked, suddenly tired of all the secrets.

"What? Who on earth told you that?"

She avoided my eyes, instead focusing on tidying the plates away. "Son, you have had a long day. Go and get some rest and do some studying. You have not opened your books for weeks now…"

"Mother…"

"Do not argue with me and do as I say!" she snapped. Although she was angry she could not hide the wild fear in her eyes. She never told me the whole story while information kept oozing from other sources. I was angry at her.

Settling into bed that night, I tried to understand what Mother was afraid of. Had Uncle threatened her somehow? She was a single mother after all, trying her hardest to bring up a son who seemed to be good for nothing except getting himself into trouble. I lay in my bed but couldn't sleep, thinking about how lonely I felt. There was no place for me. If my people discovered I was a spy, I would be chased out of the camp, or even worse, killed. My best friend was missing, God knows where. He had left me here by myself, forcing me to solve a mystery that no one else seemed to care about and was only getting me into more trouble. Not even my own mother was able to help me.

I went to my book and looked at Father's picture again, crying silently and asking him where he was. That night in May 1993, I did not want to grow up. As usual, I fell asleep with destruction around me, my heart cold with hopelessness.

Ahmed came back a week later. The news of his return spread through the camp like wildfire. I convinced Mr. Khalil to let me out of school early so I could see him before classes were over and the rest of the school showed up at his house. However, there were already lots of people inside and outside the house. It was more crowded than the average demonstration. I pushed my way through the crowds until I finally found him sitting in the living room. He stood up immediately when he noticed me and walked towards me with a big smile on his face and gave me a big hug. I couldn't remember the last time I was so happy.

"I bet you can score lots of goals now with your bendy foot!" he said laughing.

"Just like that new Man U player. What's his name, Beckham?"

We hugged for a long time as everyone around us smiled. Abu Ahmed walked by and patted us on the shoulder. He was so happy to see us both reunited.

Soumaya approached us, wearing a headscarf for the first time and offering us fizzy orange drinks as was the habit at celebration times. She looked different in the headscarf. She was now sixteen years old. I could not help noticing how her small breasts were beginning to show underneath the black t-shirt she was wearing. She was alive with laughter and her cheeks were rosy; I had never realised how pretty she was. She kept glancing over at her brother as she circled the party with her drinks, almost as if she was terrified someone would try and steal him again.

Uncle appeared too, but stayed briefly this time. He came to congratulate the family on Ahmed's safe return and left as he told me that he would tell Mother that I would be staying the night there. Even though that had been my intention, I hated hearing him talk like this. It was as if he was giving me his permission and that I was following his orders, as if he was my father. My foul mood did not last long though, as one of Ahmed's aunts had prepared a feast of stuffed aubergines, courgettes and vine leaves. I watched Ahmed attack the food before him as if he had just finished a hunger strike. It was one of the happiest meals of my life.

That night, Ahmed, Soumaya and I were left on our own as the others went to sleep. Soumaya kept stroking her brother's hair and asking lots of questions about how he got arrested, but he hardly answered any of them. It wasn't until she had finally gone to bed that he told me what had happened. The day after he came to see me in hospital and saw how angry Uncle was with me, Ahmed spotted Uncle Attiya in Jabalia getting into a taxi heading to Gaza City. He was surprised to see him get in the car instead of being at work. Quickly, Ahmed jumped in the next taxi and followed Uncle. He kept an eye on him until he ducked into Darraj Solicitors Office for Land Dispute. Waiting outside, Ahmed considered going in immediately after Uncle left to try find out what had been discussed. He had no idea how he was going to get the information out of them, being only a boy of twelve, but he was desperate enough to try. But to his bad fortune, as soon as Uncle left the solicitors shut the office for the afternoon as it was coming to 2pm.

Not knowing what else to do, Ahmed decided to carry on following Uncle. Perhaps he could find something else of use to the investigation. They headed back to Jabalia and Uncle went to Othman's Translation Office and then to a neighbour's house. Another taxi ride took them north of Jabalia out to Beit Lahia Town, through Beit Hanoun and then very close to the Erez Crossing with Gaza. Losing his nerve, Ahmed got out of the taxi and walked along the barbed wire on the no-man's-land side of the border and carried on towards the beach. He had not walked far before an Israeli military jeep suddenly appeared out of nowhere. They stopped him and some pointed their guns at his head while others brought search dogs out of the jeep. The dogs started to explore the area he had walked across. They gave him a body search and finally chucked him into the back of the jeep. He was arrested for a week before he was finally released and thrown out at the Erez Border Crossing and had to walk all the way home.

He finished talking as I stared at him, feeling sorry and responsible for what had happened to him. That night I thought about what the grown-ups had been talking about all day, the peace agreement. I did not understand all the details, but I lay there and wondered how peace could possibly last in a place like this? There was no hope, no future to look forward to. I was just a child but even I knew that, while people like me existed, there was no hope for my people. I had become poisonous to those around me. That night, I decided once and for all to end my collaboration with Uri and the whole of the damn Israeli army.

9

That summer I started noticing and thinking about girls. The worst part was that I was thinking a lot more about Soumaya and what I would do if I managed to get her alone. I started to convince myself that she had feelings for me too, even though she was at least four years older – the daydream made me happy. While I secretly enjoyed my fantasy of being locked in a room with Soumaya, I felt guilty for having such thoughts about my best friend's sister, ashamed I could think something like that.

One day, after Friday prayer in the El-Khulafa Mosque, I went to the Imam and asked him if God would throw me into hell for having such thoughts. I did not want to reveal names of course so as not to get into trouble. Nonetheless, the Imam was horrified and blessed me several times, praying that I would be guided back to the righteous path. He asked me to read the Quran daily because, he said, the devil that had been sent to corrupt my soul seemed strong and the only way to get rid of him was to read more passages from the holy Quran, as the angels would descend from heaven and fend off any devil in the room. I listened to him, bewildered at the idea there was something greater than the Israeli army to fear. I was not entirely sure whether I believed him or not, but I found it reassuring to know there was a greater power than the Israeli army and Uri. My hatred towards Uri grew by the day, resenting the moment Mr. Khalil would pass me another message from him.

Mother noticed my sudden turn to religion and wondered what had brought about this change. She even came to school to speak to the headmaster, wondering whether I had been bullied into it or if Hamas had managed to recruit me. Mother never liked either of the main political parties, saying that they both used either religion or nationalism to control the minds of their followers. She believed that fighting for the homeland and for our right to exist had nothing to do with religion. She always said: "You could be any religion you want and at the same time have the right to assert your national identity." To her, the Palestinian cause was not religious but a national one.

Finally, that fateful day in September 1993, the one no one believed would ever come, arrived. We watched our leader, Yasser Arafat, sitting in the White House with Yitzhak Rabin, the Israeli prime minister at the time, Bill Clinton, the US president and his Secretary of State Madeleine Albright. We waited for the hasty handshake and cheered when it finally happened. Mother screamed at the top of her voice, blasting the TV up at full volume, the sound drowned out by the other TVs in the neighbourhood. Everyone was celebrating.

"What are you happy about Mother? This is not going to change much. Why couldn't we have just waited a bit longer and negotiated better?"

"Celebrate now, reflect later," she replied as she clapped her hands.

"Mother!"

"Omar, think of it as a ceasefire, and not a solution. I know how you feel and many will agree with you. But think about it: People are eager for some peace. Over the last week no one was killed and that, in itself, is a major breakthrough. People throw stones not because they enjoy it, but because they want to stand up to the soldiers and make their voices heard. Well, whether by stones or by signing a peace agreement, we are still doing that."

The weeks that followed the signing were very difficult. It was announced that a newly formed Palestinian Authority would come to Gaza and Jericho to start taking on the responsibilities of self-rule. Yasser Arafat and his advisers were giving interviews to the international media about how they would govern the Gaza Strip, appointing people as ministers and officials. With the new hope and enthusiasm people woke up with every day now, the Israelis were even more determined to make people's lives harder than ever, while they still could. They intensified their raids and there was a daily curfew from 8pm. There were many arrests and of course, to my disgust, more work for me.

By December, the plan for the Israeli withdrawal from the Gaza Strip became public knowledge; however, no one knew when the official military withdrawal date was. The Israeli settlements in Gaza would be staying. The soldiers wanted to make sure to cleanse the tiny Strip of any form of resistance; assassinating leaders and arresting those who they thought might continue to give them trouble. One day, Mr. Khalil passed me a message through the usual notebook trick I had now become familiar with. There was a little note that had the name Hussam Awwad scribbled on it and instructions to report information of his activities back to Mr. Khalil. The note made it clear that this was an important operation, stressing my information had to be accurate; the time he left the house, which places he visited, who he hung out with, which shops he went to, were all important.

As I walked home from school that day, I wondered who Hussam Awwad was. I had never heard about him or seen him anywhere. The address in the note told me that his house was not too far from mine, about six blocks away from Sanaida Street.

I could not wait for Uri and the Israelis to leave the damned camp and never return. I was frustrated by everyone around me, but mostly I was just angry with myself. This time I remembered Mother's story about the donkey and how he went back for his death the second time. I refused to end up like that donkey. Enough was enough. I couldn't be responsible for another person's death. I did not know who Hussam was, but pictured him as a young father, whose children would one day seek out revenge against their father's killer. Me.

But what should I do now? I was expected to provide the information in a week's time. What would happen to me if I did not give them what they wanted? The answer made me shiver especially when I remembered what Uri did to me in his office. But even faced with death, I knew I could not do it anymore. I was a dead man, no longer an innocent boy, and no one could help me.

I walked and walked, circling the camp several times as I tried to figure out what I should do next, even though I knew there was nothing that could be done to save me. Eventually my feet led me back home, where Um Marwan was in her usual place with a small fire lit next to her to keep the December chill away.

"Hello, Omar," she called as she saw me.

I stopped to acknowledge her but could not even feign a smile. She looked grimly at me, getting up from her spot and approaching me slowly.

"Omar. What is wrong? What is troubling you?"

A painful lump gathered in my throat and I could not trust myself to answer, instead shaking my head.

"Omar, is there something wrong? You can tell me. I can try and help you."

I shook my head again, "You cannot."

She considered me for a moment, then put an arm around my shoulder.

"Let's go inside."

Her husband was out playing backgammon as usual. The house was cold and quiet. She got a blanket out for me as I sat on the mattress in her living room, then went to the kitchen to boil a pot of tea.

The steam of the cup was very comforting to watch in the candlelight. As soon as I had my first sip and looked at Um Marwan's worried eyes, I broke down in tears. I could not help myself. I did not know where to start or what to say to her. But eventually, in a broken voice, I managed to tell her everything. From the moment I went to Uri, to the note I had received that day. At first, she was puzzled. She shook her head when I confessed about Zuheir's death, our lovely neighbour who was my first victim of collaboration with the enemy. By the time I had finished, she wasn't looking at me anymore. She stared at the floor, shaking her head and moaning softly.

"No, No… That can't be…"

I did not dare answer her; instead I curled up underneath the blanket, keeping half of my face covered. It was getting darker and colder outside. I was shivering, but I was not sure whether it was the temperature or my fear. I had finally told someone. A small part of me felt as if a burden had been lifted off my shoulders, and it felt good that I had confessed everything to someone, even though Um Marwan would no doubt throw me out of her house.

Um Marwan finally stood up and stared down at me. Finally, she pulled the blanket back from me.

"Right, you are coming with me now. Leave your school bag here."

"Where are we going?"

"You will see," she said, tugging at my arm. We left the house and walked in the cover of darkness. There was only half an hour left before the curfew started and I began feeling uneasy. I couldn't see where we were going but from the turns we took I knew we were going to the Fakhoura area in the north of the Jabalia Camp; it was a cloudy night, making it darker than usual.

We finally turned left off the main Fakhoura road and down a small lane, leaving behind the faint lights of candles coming from several windows in the area. We headed down a small sandy lane, the smell of cacti and oranges very powerful. I could almost tell the type of tree from their shadows. The lane was long, we must have walked for about fifteen minutes before we finally approached a big house with several windows lit with candles. Um Marwan knocked hard on the front door and then turned to face me.

"Right, you do not say anything now. Let me talk. Do you hear me?"

"Yes," I said, heart pumping.

A masked man opened the door and ushered us in. I could feel his eyes on me as I tried to make myself as invisible as possible behind Um Marwan. She continued to pull me along until we reached a big living room. The first thing that caught my eye was the big portrait of Yasser Arafat that covered the front wall. There was very little furniture, with an empty sofa, a wooden coffee table and two mattresses in the other corner of the room. I noticed that the room had no windows.

We both sat on the sofa and waited until a group of masked men walked in carrying prayer mats and beads. A couple carried rifles. They stopped as they saw us. One reached for his gun, but a tall, masked man with a big belly stopped him.

"*Ahlan*, Um Marwan. Welcome. *Keef Halek*? How are you doing?" asked a short person who headed towards the mattresses on the floor, pulling out his pistol as he did so.

"I am afraid I am very troubled."

"Oh dear. What can we do for you?"

The masked man who opened the door for us was offering her coffee. She held it tightly in her hand as she waited for everyone to be served. Once the man headed back to the kitchen and everyone had settled on the mattress, Um Marwan got up quickly and approached the short man, who I guess was probably their leader. She put the coffee down close to his foot.

"I will not drink your coffee until you promise to listen to me and help me. Well, not me, but him. That boy. You need to promise."

In our tradition, this was a big gesture. It was considered offensive for someone to refuse the host's coffee. The man could see that Um Marwan was serious in her desperation, but instead of being insulted, he smiled as he passed her cup back to her.

"Drink, Um Marwan and everything will be okay if God wills it."

She drank and then slowly began to tell them my story. I was glad she remembered everything so well, as I could not bring myself to speak in this company. But the moment she finished, I heard guns being loaded. Suddenly I was being kicked to the ground by one of the men while another grabbed some rope to tie me up and another put duct tape over my mouth.

"Stop it. Stop it right now!" Um Marwan was shouting, tears in her eyes. "Shame on you! This is why the Palestinian cause is lost because people like you have no honour left! Is this how you treat a boy? Why are you not this brave with the Israeli soldiers, you swine."

"Um Marwan, how do you know he is not spying on us right now? How do you know he is not going to give them our location? Who knows they might already be on their way," one of the men shouted as his panic rose.

"I did not force him to talk," Um Marwan said. "He trusted me. There is no one coming."

"Remove the tape from his mouth," the leader ordered sharply.

The tape was ripped mercilessly from my mouth, causing blood to start dripping from my lips. He then came close and put the gun against my head.

"Tell me boy, is there anyone coming here tonight?"

I shook my head, but he put his finger on the trigger anyway.

"I am going to ask one more time, and I want you to look me in the eye and answer. Is there anyone coming here tonight?"

"No, I swear by almighty Allah. There is no one coming. Please, please either believe me or shoot me. I cannot take it anymore."

Tears were falling on my cheeks, I was beyond the point of fear. The reality was that I no longer cared if he shot me. I just wanted it to be all over.

The masked man with the big belly whispered something to the short leader. The leader retreated and went back to his seat on the mattress, motioning for the rest of his men to do the same. Um Marwan looked relieved as she hugged me close, then began to untie me.

"Not so fast Um Marwan," the leader called. "Tell me boy, how did you get your orders from the Israelis?"

His gun was still pointing at us as he asked. I did not expect his question and suddenly realised I had not thought that through enough. Yet again, I was endangering someone else's life because I was trying to save myself.

"Answer the fucking question, or I will blow your head off. I don't think anyone here would feel sorry for you after what you've done. Betray your own people, eh? And for what? Did they pay you?"

"No," I mumbled.

"Did they get your father back?"

"No."

"Then why the hell did you continue giving them information?"

"I was frightened."

"Of what?"

I was saved from answering by Um Marwan who had suddenly had enough. She launched herself at him and began shaking him violently. The others were stunned for a moment, then closed in around them, waiting for their orders.

"I saved your arse more than once and this is how you repay me," Um Marwan screamed. "Had I known you were that cruel, I would have let the Israeli dogs eat your flesh or left you to rot somewhere. Shame on you."

The leader broke Um Marwan's grip on him but ordered his men back. He straightened his clothes as he glared at me.

"You are lucky, boy. I owe this woman a lot. Had she not been with you, I would have blown your head off. Now answer my question and no harm will be done. I give you my word."

Um Marwan looked at me with pleading eyes, but I did not want to mention Mr. Khalil's name. I thought of how he was bullied at the border to become a spy, and the hard decision he had to make between his son or his country. I thought of his goddaughter probably somewhere in the US, no doubt very proud of him.

"Tell them, Omar. Don't be a fool," Um Marwan pleaded.

Once again, I had been forced to destroy someone's life.

"Mr. Khalil, my geography teacher. He would pass notes to me that carried my instructions. He passed me the note today. It's in my pocket."

Someone searched my pocket and got the note out. The moment he read out the name, silence fell in the room. Even Um Marwan looked apprehensive.

"Do you know who that guy is Omar?" the leader asked, his voice softer than before.

"No, never heard of him."

"Hussam Awwad is the leader of northern Gaza Operations of Fatah."

This meant nothing to me and I did not bother to hide my blank stare.

"They want to get him because he opposed the Oslo agreement. Listen, Omar, you are a brave boy to come here today. There is perhaps still time to fix things and put them right. I am sure you will agree that Uri is an evil person. This is why we fight, because of what they have done to our people and what they continue to do, to people like you."

He was now speaking softly and more gently. I could only see his eyes through the mask but somehow at that moment they looked very gentle. Yet I was afraid that they would start torturing me after this smooth talk.

"That bastard Uri has abused your childhood and that of many others. Listen, Omar, we have to get him. We have to punish the bastard for what he has done."

I couldn't agree more with that, in fact my mouth was wide-open smiling as if I was ready to start chanting my demonstration chants. But something told me there will be more abuse to come.

"Here is the plan, Omar. You will write back to Mr. Khalil and tell him that you have information on Hussam, but that you must tell Uri in person. Tell him it is too dangerous and important to trust it to anyone else, something that cannot be covered in a small note. Ask to meet the General alone in Tel El-Zaatar, behind the sandy hill before the barbed wire. Stress the importance of him coming alone and not being recognised, as people have started to suspect you may be an informant. Ask him to come on Wednesday night straight after evening prayer. When he arrives, we will be waiting for him."

"What if he doesn't turn up?" I asked.

"Then no harm done, we will just think of something else. Now, I could be making a mistake of trusting you here and sending you home, but out of my respect for Um Marwan, I am going to take the risk." There was murmur from the other men but he ignored them. "Go, before I change my mind."

Someone cut my bonds and pushed me towards Um Marwan, who led me back through the living room and out of the house, rushing through the lane. We walked back to our house, my mind was full of different thoughts. I wanted to atone for my actions and become a hero, but couldn't stop thinking that that was too risky. Luckily, there were no Israeli military jeeps to notice that we were breaking the curfew. Um Marwan knocked on our door violently, as Mother opened startled.

"Where have you been?" she demanded, looking at Um Marwan.

"I am sorry. I took him to visit my sister in the Twam and we got caught in the curfew. We just managed our way back through the alleyways. I must go before the soldiers come. Goodnight."

She turned around and left without looking at me.

As soon as she left, Mother forcefully said, "You do not go with that woman anywhere again without telling me, is that understood! I was worried sick."

"Yes, Mother… Sorry." I avoided her glare and made my way through the darkness, finding my room and immediately collapsing onto my bed. I intended to rest only for a few minutes but I did not take long to give into my exhaustion and I fell asleep in my school uniform.

I woke up in the middle of the night when the electricity came back on; the sound of the TV that had been left on when the power went, brought me back. I turned it off and headed to the bathroom. In the mirror I saw the stains of blood on my mouth and was relieved to know that Mother hadn't noticed in the darkness. I washed and headed back to bed.

Before I left for school in the morning, Um Marwan knocked on the door again and passed Mother my school bag. I came running to the door, but only caught her eye as she turned around and winked at me. That day, I wrote the note to Mr. Khalil asking for a meeting with Uri in the specified place. He read it on the spot and in front of all the unsuspecting kids, then he stared at me for a long time, but I just moved my head up and down begging him to agree to pass on my request.

10

Two hours to go before 6:30pm on Wednesday 15th of December, 1993. My body had been shaking all day. I had skipped school, I was too worried, this could be the day that I would finally be liberated and become a normal person again – accepted within this cursed society – or it could simply be the last day of my life. Either way, by the end of the day I would have closure. Even if Uri didn't turn up, I would liberate myself from his threats. The resistance knew about what I did and he could not bully me into supplying him with more information. Suddenly, a feeling of euphoria filled my body; somehow things would turn out well enough.

After prayers, the Imam stopped me to have a chat about my sexual thoughts and invited me to go up to the mosque's office. Instead, I excused myself as quickly and politely as I could, laughing to myself at this man who was so obsessed with trying to cleanse people of their 'sins'. The truth was that I hadn't had these thoughts for a while. Not because I read the Quran, as he had recommended, but simply because my life was at stake. I left the mosque after prayers, and as I headed towards the sandy hill of Tel Al-Zaatar, it started to drizzle. The rain made it exceptionally cold. I shivered as I made my way up the hill and as I stood there waiting, the rain got heavier. Soon I was soaking. Then I saw car headlights in the distance. I descended the hill to the middle of the square which was normally used as a football pitch by the local kids; it was wide enough and surrounded by buildings from the other side, with no main road and without many nasty neighbours to tell them off when they argued loudly about the scores.

I stood in the middle of the square as I saw Uri's tall silhouette approach me. I nervously glanced around. I could not see any masked men. I suddenly began to worry that they had forgotten the whole thing. Was it a trap to get me killed at the hands of the Israelis? Uri continued to advance towards me, hands in his pockets. My heart was pounding, not knowing what to do. I had no information to give him. How was I going to get away now?

The only flaw in the plan was that the trap wasn't there. It was only me. Just before Uri got to me he suddenly stopped and looked around. Then he turned and started running back to his car as a sudden hail of bullets descended upon him. I was thrilled at the sight of that bastard running away like a proper coward. He shouted in Hebrew, when he suddenly fell on the ground. He was shot.

There was a moment of silence and then bullets started flying again as he got up and limped as fast as he could towards his car. Bullets continued to fly everywhere as I watched the car's headlight switch on and heard the engine rev. Before I knew he was gone.

I could hear curses from the masked men as they appeared behind me. Someone was shouting and another one called his friend an idiot for not being able to aim properly. Others were already trying to decide what the next step would be. But I was already running. At the moment, the only thought on my mind was Mr. Khalil. Not only had I handed him over to the resistance, I had also made him lie to Uri, who would now think that he was involved in the ploy too. The Israelis would not let him live after this betrayal.

I ran through the alleys of the Jabalia Camp, praying that the soldiers would not run into me during curfew. When I finally reached El-Juron, where Mr. Khalil lived, I slammed my fist on the door. He answered the door in his pyjamas and was startled to see me outside at that hour.

"You must leave. Now!" I shouted at him.

"Leave? Where to? What happened?"

I told him everything as I pushed him inside, quickly finding his wardrobe and throwing some clothes out for him.

"One of them will kill you," I said, pushing the clothes into a rucksack I had found. "You need to escape while you still can."

He said nothing. His hands shook as he searched for his crutches that had been buried beneath the pile of clothes. Once he was ready, I helped carry his bag out, closing his front door behind us once we were facing the bitter cold air.

"It's time to go now," I said, handing him the bag. "Go. Quickly."

His eyes, wide with terror, considered me for a second, before he gathered me with one arm for a brief hug. Then I watched him as he started limping his way up the street, letting the darkness envelop him.

I knew that Uri would be looking for me by now and wanted to say goodbye to Mother before I too disappeared. I ran back to our street as fast as I could, pausing at the last corner to look around for any military jeeps that Uri might have sent to find me at home. It was very quiet. Taking the risk, I crossed our street and headed home. Just before I reached our front door, two masked men stopped me, one putting his hand over my mouth to prevent me from making any noise.

Instead of taking me inside, they led me to the end of the street to Mohammed El-Balbisi's house. We headed to the kitchen, where the first masked man pushed a barrel of flour across the floor, revealing a trap door. As he began to squeeze his way inside, the other man pushed me forward, forcing me to go before him. The tunnel was narrow, with barely enough room for any of us to fit our heads. The second man closed the trap door behind him, plunging us all into temporary darkness before the first man managed to locate his torch. Crawling along on our stomachs, we began what felt like a painfully slow journey along the tunnel, turning corners occasionally and scratching our hands on the rock and debris on the floor. Eventually my knees started to bleed while my nose was filled with the stink of sewage and dead rats.

At one point I suddenly froze, ignoring the curses of the man behind me. Mother did not know where I was. She would be expecting me for dinner. I realised the masked men had prevented me from going home so as to not endanger her life, but my eyes began to tear up as I realised that I may never see her again.

As my tears continued to fall, I was unable to move, the man behind me lost his patience.

"Come on, hurry. No time to waste."

I realised that he was not being mean. He was trying to help by being brusque, to shake me back into myself. I sniffed and tried my best to get going again, ignoring the pain in my hands and knees.

We finally got to a turning where the only way forward was up. I closed my tired eyes in silent thankfulness. I could not have continued for much longer. The man in front knocked on the trap door three times, waited for a moment, then knocked once and then another two times. The door opened and, to my amazement and relief, I saw the familiar face of Um Marwan, peering down at us.

The tunnel had led us to a house I had never seen before. We got out by the kitchen that was stocked with barrels of flour, rice, sugar, olives and pickles. The living room was no tidier than the kitchen. There were lots of second-hand telephones scattered around the floor, seatbelts ripped from cars, cushions upside down.

"You are going to stay here for a while Omar," Um Marwan told me. "It is not safe for you anymore out there."

"I understand. Thank you."

"You were very brave, little one. Your father would have been very proud of you."

This was not as comforting as it perhaps would have been once. It was my mission to find Father that had led me here, to this horrible position.

"Is Uri dead?"

My question was met with silence, which either meant they did not know, or that he had survived.

"Omar..." Um Marwan said handing me a *kufiyyah* scarf, "you are going to have to cover your face with this from now on."

"You are one of us now," one of the masked men said, his eyes glittering in the candle-lit room.

I sat holding the *kufiyyah* in my hand, watching Um Marwan put on her headscarf, getting ready to leave. One of my companions was resting on the mattress, crossing his legs as he leaned his back to the wall and leaving his pistol right in front of him. I was not sure whether I was being imprisoned, but I was stuck here either way. It was not safe to go back home.

"I will tell your mother that you are safe," Um Marwan said as she turned to leave.

"How long will I be here?"

"I am not sure, Omar. Until things calm down a bit. We will see. But you will be safe here."

"Yes, of course, I will look after you," my masked companion said. "You will have to wear that scarf if you want to leave. However, you cannot go anywhere near your home, masked or not. Do you understand?"

He continued to give me instructions, as Um Marwan disappeared. There was only one windowless room in the house where we could turn a light on, the rest had to stay dark. Food could only be cooked during the day, so that the light from the cooker wouldn't show in the dark. Tea or coffee could be made in the daylight and saved in two large flasks. There was no heating and fire was not allowed; we would have to make do with the plentiful of blankets they had. There was a small portable Sony radio player that had to be kept low. The maximum volume allowed was marked clearly with a small piece of blue tape.

I sat there listening to all the instructions, trying to take them all in. Finally, he asked if I had any questions.

"Where are we?"

"I will show you in the morning. No doubt you will recognise where you are," he said as he took his pistol apart and began to clean it with a cloth. "Do you know how to use this?"

"No, we didn't study weapon handling at school."

He laughed loudly at this, which made me nervous. He had a distinctive laugh and a high-pitched voice that made him sound like one of those evil jinns from the *One Thousand and One Nights.*

"Well, consider this school from now on. You will not be able to go to classes anymore. In fact you will not be able to go anywhere the Israelis might look for you."

I had not thought of school, having been so concerned about Mother. Uncle had always told me how important it was to be educated and encouraged me to get the best marks. He told me that my weak body would not stand a life of hardship or the working conditions on construction sites in Gaza or in Israel, and that my brain was made for office work or perhaps even a leadership position somewhere. But now, all of these dreams were lost.

The house we were in was half destroyed. In the morning, I walked through the other rooms and found rubble on the eastern side of the house. As I tripped over broken stones, I found a naked doll with a broken arm and long brown hair, a deflated ball and a half burned copy of *Kalila wa Dimna.* The illustrations were comforting to look at, even though most of the writing had been destroyed. I sat down after pouring a lukewarm cup of tea from one of the flasks and tried to fill in the gaps of the story from memory.

I recognised one of my favourite tales about a curious monkey and his owner, the carpenter, who lived together happily. The carpenter took his monkey on walks every day after work and introduced him to all his friends. During the day, the monkey watched his owner making doors, windows, wardrobes and desks. When the carpenter left for lunch, the monkey would try to create the same things, holding the hammer and banging on the planks of wood, pretending to be useful. The carpenter often warned the monkey not to interfere in his work, saying that "he who interfered in someone else's business often discovered things that they did not like." But the monkey would not listen. One day, after the carpenter left him alone, the monkey saw two large planks of wood laid next to each other on a high workbench, wedged together by pieces of wood.

The monkey stuck his head between the two planks, wondering why they had been wedged together like that. He was sure that his owner was tired that day and the aim was to create one big plank to make a gate. He decided to help his owner by removing the wedges. What he didn't realise was that the two planks were being pressed by two powerful springs and the moment he removed the wedges the two planks came rushing towards the monkey's neck. When the carpenter came home, he found the monkey dead. As he mourned his death, the news spread in the neighbourhood and the saying "he who interferes in someone else's business often finds things they don't like" became a famous Arabic proverb.

Over the next few months, I tried to get into some sort of routine. My companion talked a lot but he never removed his mask. He taught me how to put mine on whenever I decided to go out. The house was in El-Juron area in Jabalia Town that was adjacent to the Jabalia Refugee Camp. The area still had olive groves and the house was hidden in one of them, behind lots of dead tree trunks, rubble and some junk. It was near invisible from a distance and even from up-close it looked more like a dump and smelled rotten. It was a safe place for my guard and me to lay low. The door was left unlocked, as masked men would wander in at night to rest and plan their operations. The short leader came at least once a week and the man with the big belly came more often, at least twice a week.

I missed Mother painfully but did not dare to go anywhere near her. I missed the warmth of my bed, the smell of her food.

I would have done anything to see Mother, but my instructions were clear; I was not to venture anywhere near our street. We needed to give the Israelis the impression that I had left the Gaza Strip all together, just as Mr. Khalil had. There was no room for error, otherwise I would jeopardise the resistance even further.

"Don't fuck it up Omar," my companion warned me one morning about a week after my arrival, when I let slip my yearnings for home. "You've done us enough harm already. It is now time to correct things. You are one of us."

It was funny talking to someone wearing a mask all the time. It was almost like talking to a ghost. Most of the masked men never removed their masks and often referred to each other as Abu something or other, rather than their real names.

"What about you Omar?" one eventually asked. "What shall we call you? Abu what?"

"Abu Mustafa," I replied without hesitation. I had often thought that, if I ever had a son, I would name him after Father. Since my future now seemed set against this possibility, I took my father's name instead. My companion was known as Abu Hammad.

As the weeks passed, he started teaching me how to use a gun, first by cleaning it and putting it together. We then moved to aiming and later to shooting. We had to choose our times carefully so as not to attract the attention of the Israeli soldiers. Possessing a gun was a crime that could result in a life sentence, as well as the Israelis destroying the house of the owner. We could not risk being captured. We practiced in the dark and walked for miles through the olive groves to get to the beach. After two months, I was being trained almost every night in shooting or martial arts or riding horses or whatever else Abu Hammad considered a useful skill to possess. By February 1994 I had mastered all those skills, becoming agile, growing taller and building muscle. At the age of thirteen, my facial hair started to appear. I was becoming a man.

Though Abu Hammad started to trust me, he never removed his mask or told me his real name. He often woke up screaming in the middle of the night, scaring me to death. I would grab my gun and run to his room where I would find him sweating and shaking. Giving him a cup of tea always seemed to calm him down. Over the time we spent together, I got to know him a little better. He was married with six children who lived somewhere in the Gaza Strip, though he would not reveal where. He used to work as a doctor for the UNRWA medical practice. He treated many patients on a daily basis and occasionally Israeli soldiers who collapsed nearby from sunstroke. His parents and siblings lived in the West Bank town of Hebron and he would visit them often, sometimes once a week. They had a large six-bedroom house built from old Jerusalem stones and a beautiful garden that had lots of apricot and almond trees, as well as a beautiful vine that produced the sweetest grapes.

Abu Hammad had studied medicine in Jordan and decided to move to Gaza to help refugees. He believed in the potential to create a national front to defend Palestinian rights. Returning home one day, he noticed rubbish outside his house. The windows had been broken and what looked like barbed wire now covered the roof. He knocked on the front door and was met by the back of an M16 rifle that knocked him down, his nose bleeding profusely.

The Israeli settler pointed the gun directly at him. "*Tse Hahotsa*. Get out of here!" he shouted at him in Hebrew, as two other similar-looking settlers came to the door holding their rifles.

"*Hada Beiti*, this is my home!" Abu Hammad had shouted back at them before one of them fired their gun in the air, sending my companion running for his life. One of the neighbours stopped him and told him that the settlers had moved there a few weeks ago.

He learned that the settlers had killed his mother and two of his siblings as they took over their house. The rest of his family were put in jail for trying to take their home back.

Abu Hammad went to the Israeli High Court to plead for justice, but his appeal fell on deaf ears. He was not even allowed to visit his family in prison, as he was refused a permit to enter Israel. He returned back to Gaza and two weeks later, he had joined the resistance.

11

He was led by a short Egyptian police officer wearing a stained white uniform, a thin man walking nervously ahead of Omar as if he was about to be stabbed in the back. He kept shouting at his Palestinian deportee, insulting Omar for not keeping up with him. They went through the immigration desk, then right into the departure hall until they got to the airline desks, where they stopped at the Royal Jordanian section. Omar had his credit card ready, hoping that it would work despite not having informed HSBC that he was travelling that day. He handed it nervously, hoping that it would get him booked for the 6pm flight and back again to Cairo on the 10pm flight.

Within minutes everything was booked and both of them were rushing through to get to the departure gate with one hour left for the plane to leave.

"I am going to Jordan now and back again later this evening." He was almost shouting on the phone as he jogged his way through the crowd of people.

"Why?" Zoe's tired voice came through.

"Don't know, don't ask, that's what I was told to do. Nothing makes sense in this part of the world, but it is all sorted out. Could I ask you for a favour? Can you log in to our online account and register my trip with the bank? I am worried I won't be able to use my cards here anymore."

"Sure...my love, I miss you," Omar could almost feel the warmth of her tears. Sadness took over him and he could hardly move. The policeman stopped in the middle of the airport and started shouting at him. Everyone around stared at the scene.

"I've got to go Zoe...I will be back...I promise." He hung up the phone not knowing whether he would be able to keep his promise or not. This war on Gaza was different than any other, it had been going for four weeks now and nearly two thousand people have been killed. He knew that he could be targeted any minute and that he may never see his wife and child again. But there was no other way, he had to get to Gaza. He tried to call his uncle's house once more but there was no answer. He then texted Ahmed and waited for a long time without any reply. The police officer told him that he had heard on the news that a ceasefire was likely to take place in the morning on the first day of August. So if Omar was lucky, the border should open once he returns from Jordan.

As he got to the plane, he thought of little Mustafa getting in the bath and how much he loved the water, soaking the whole floor while splashing wildly. Omar smiled as he imagined Mustafa's little body kicking the water so hard as his mummy came to tell him off for making such a mess. But suddenly the smile was gone when Omar realised that his son might grow up like him searching for his father. And like him, Mustafa might not understand much about why his father disappeared.

On the plane, Omar picked up his notebook again and started writing. He didn't know when Mustafa would read this and whether he would understand everything. He wrote a couple of pages and then deleted them, and then he started all over again, not knowing how to make it easier for his son to understand everything. Suddenly, he thought of another story from Kalila and Dimna and he started writing.

"Once upon a time, there was a wise Imam who was known for his good character. Everyone loved him and asked for his advice on

all matters regarding their lives. He could always see a way through problems, finding the positive side of things. The King loved him too and consulted him occasionally. He refused to move to the King's palace permanently, as the King wished, preferring the simple life of his village. He was married to a beautiful woman who, like him, was idolised in the village and loved by all the women. The happy couple worked in the local mosques together, giving lectures on morality and helping with the paperwork for all the villagers without ever asking for a penny, for they had everything in life they needed.

"What they did not have, however, was a child. They tried everything they could, including herbal medicine and seeing physicians who came from the Farsi land. The Imam had a pet meerkat and loved it dearly, taking it everywhere with him. People said that the Imam loved his pet almost as much as people loved their children. The meerkat also loved the Imam and was incredibly loyal to him. It would jump up and down whenever it saw its owner. It would not sleep until it was sure that the Imam and his wife were fast asleep first, snoring loudly in their bed.

"They lived like this for a long time, until one day, by some miracle, the Imam's wife became pregnant and gave birth to a beautiful son they called Mohammed. The Imam loved his son very much and spent all his time with him. The meerkat also loved the baby and would guard him faithfully, even though the Imam began to neglect the meerkat. One day, the Imam's wife had to go help the women get water for the mosque. She kissed her husband and child goodbye and left. As the Imam started playing with his son, a messenger knocked on the door and told him that the King had sent for him urgently. The Imam was worried about his son, but decided that he would go quickly as his son was asleep and would be back before the baby was awake. To reassure him, the meerkat immediately dashed to the child's side and looked at the Imam as if to say, 'don't worry, I am here.' As soon as the Imam left, the meerkat began his vigil. A few minutes later a giant snake suddenly

appeared, making its way towards the baby. The meerkat attacked at once, biting and scratching the snake until finally, after a desperate struggle, the snake lay dead. When the Imam returned, the meerkat ran to greet him, proud of itself for defending his son. But when the Imam saw the blood on the meerkat's mouth, he assumed that the meerkat had attacked his son out of jealousy. Outraged and heartbroken, the Imam swooped down on the meerkat and killed it with his bare hands. But when he saw his son sound asleep and the dead snake next to him, he realised the horrible mistake he had made. From that day on, the Imam always wore black and never mentioned the meerkat again. He left the village with his family soon after and was never seen again."

My first order as a newly recruited freedom fighter came in March 1994, four months before the expected arrival of Yasser Arafat, the president of the newly formed Palestinian Authority. Those were tense months, as the Israeli soldiers were leaving Gaza at a time when a lot of PLO Officials were arriving to pave the way for the arrival of Mr. Arafat. Therefore, both the resistance's work and the Israelis' had intensified in order to gain as much advantages as possible in this turbulent period. First, I was asked to be on look out for a group of masked men who were attempting to plant a bomb on the road between Al-Nusairat and Deir El-Balah. When the bomb had been detonated and the Israeli tank exploded, we retreated to our house in El-Juron to celebrate. There was a party mood in the house that night. But while some drank whisky and cheered, others knelt down on their knees and prayed all night. I was then asked to burn a military jeep and write slogans all over town at night. I never failed. My new Abu Mustafa nickname was becoming known in the world of resistance. They would contact me for any mission they needed and I would always oblige. It became clearer to me why these people masked themselves and decided to fight the Israelis. It was to give hope to those who had nothing left anymore.

From a self-hating collaborator to a freedom fighter, I was back with my people again. Even though I did not choose to be the hero I was made to be, it was satisfying to have some sort of purpose in life. Attacking the occupation forces, freeing our land from those bastard soldiers, was a good enough reason for me to live. Abu Hammad and I became good friends. He hardly laughed, but I learned how to read eyes; emotions existed in there; respect, fear, anxiety, satisfaction. I learned to cook and made delicious traditional dishes made with rice, couscous, aubergine and seasonal vegetables, which grew in the olive grove near us.

Um Marwan visited us every week bringing with her essential supplies of bread, vegetables and canned food, which were battered like UNRWA's food hand-outs. She looked very healthy for a woman of 73. She still had a slim athletic body, making her a quick walker. Her diet consisted mainly of olive oil and za'atar. She passed on messages to me from Mother who was missing me and desperate to come visit though she knew she could not. Um Marwan told me that our house was raided repeatedly as the Israelis searched for me. Mother was dragged out in the street and put in the back of a military jeep by no other than Uri himself. The thought of my mother being humiliated in the street like that made me sick, I almost threw up when I thought of what that bastard officer who raped me could do to my own mother. But worse, the idea that he was still alive made me angry at the people around me who had failed to kill him on that fateful night when I became homeless.

Um Marwan once brought me my Mother's signature dish, *Maglouba*, made of rice, meat and fried vegetables. The moment the smell filled my nostrils the guilt rose once more, as I thought about the pain I must have been causing her.

In June that year, the Israelis started to leave the Jabalia Camp, along with the other main camps and cities in the Strip. They retreated to settlements that were still full of Israelis, located in El-Soudania in the north, Al-Nusairat in the middle of Gaza and

Khan Younis and Rafah in the south. Crowds gathered to watch the soldiers moving out of El-Markaz, cheering and celebrating their departure. Abu Hammad and I kept our masks on and hid behind a corner far from the celebrating crowds. Some continued to throw stones as the troops paraded through the streets. The last car to leave was Uri's bulletproof military jeep. I saw him from my hiding place. He had his shades down as he glared out of the window, watching the crowd as he passed. Feeling brave, I stood out from behind the corner, making sure he could see me. It did not take long before his eyes fixed on my masked face. I removed my mask. Uri saw me and leaned out of the window for a better look. I put my middle finger up in the air, smiling as I watched his lips curse me silently, Abu Hammad laughed loudly at my side.

A week later, the leader of the resistance group came to our hiding place and informed me that I could go home if I wanted to.

"Is everyone leaving? Is this it?" I asked, relief washing over me.

"No, my little friend. Some of us will be staying. We do not all agree with this peace agreement." His sarcastic voice pierced my relief.

I looked at the men, understanding that they would struggle to go back to normal life and this was perhaps one of the reasons they felt they could not go home. Hamas was getting stronger and becoming a more popular resistance party because they disagreed with Fatah and Yasser Arafat signing the peace agreement. They made their point clear and they were now beginning to be noticed.

It didn't look like Abu Hammad was leaving either, as he embraced me tightly before I left, all the men cheering and wishing me luck as I opened the door. I walked out much different to the child that had arrived. I had done good things for my people and, for the first time in a long time, I was proud of myself. My exit was cheered by the other men as if it was a graduation event.

I walked home with the *kufiyyah* lowered on my shoulders. I wanted everyone to see me come home. I was a soldier returning from war, a victorious revolutionary – my ego growing so big that I began to believe I was responsible for driving the Israelis out of Gaza. There was a big smile on my face as I walked down our street. Um Marwan was not in her usual spot and my smile disappeared quickly the moment I saw Uncle walking up the street with his son Khalid. I tried to look fierce and put on a brave face but my cousin did not hesitate to run towards me and give me a hug. Uncle embraced me too.

"Welcome home, son."

"Don't call me 'son'. I have a father." My sharp retort startled him, and he looked at Khalid to see if he had heard, but he had already started running up the street, eager to tell his mother the good news. Uncle's eyes perused my face for a moment, uncertain of my new confidence. Finally he stepped back and patted me on the shoulder before continuing his walk. He would not treat me like I was a child again.

When I finally reached my front door and Mother found me on her doorstep, we hugged each other as if the world was about to end. Eventually she lost her balance and we both fell inside the house laughing like maniacs.

A month later, Ahmed and I took the trip down to Rafah to join people who had gathered to greet Yasser Arafat. It was the first time Ahmed and I made that journey on our own. I had missed my friend so much and was glad to have him to myself for the entire journey. He was in great spirits as we walked and chatted, both relieved I had been allowed to move on to the next year at school, despite not having been there for six months. We laughed and teased each other and argued about football all the way to the border. It was moments like these that I felt happy that things had returned to normal.

We arrived at an open space filled with people all heading to the field where the helicopter was going to land. Many of them were carrying Palestinian flags, *kufiyyahs*, posters of Yasser Arafat and pictures of their loved ones who had been killed or imprisoned. It was almost like a demonstration, except it was jovial. Everyone was laughing and some were even singing. People shouted victory slogans that charged the atmosphere with an enthusiasm that I hadn't felt from the people before. We must have walked for about two miles when we got to the field that also swarmed with people. We waited for about half an hour until we heard the sound of the helicopter coming. As soon as we spotted it, everyone started to whistle, clap and cheer, announcing the moment the whole Palestinian nation was waiting for. The helicopter came closer and closer, creating a sandstorm and forcing people to cover their eyes. We waited for a long time before Yasser Arafat finally emerged. A few people came out before him and every time the door opened the crowd cheered, but it was nothing compared to the celebration that erupted when he finally came out. It took almost a full ten minutes for the noise to die down. He was wearing his military suit with his *kufiyyah* wrapped around his head as usual. I wanted to get closer to him and so started pushing forward while Ahmed followed. It was strange. It felt as if I had known him for a long time. As if he were family or a friend of the family. Something about the way he looked was comforting.

We pushed through the crowds. It took a long time but eventually we were in the second row. I could see his face now, he looked happy. He jumped out of the helicopter like a young man, bending down on his knees and kissing the floor. As soon as he did that, shouts of *Allahu Akbar* echoed around the field. As he got up, people started playing music and some started dancing Dabke. Ahmed and I pushed through the circle of dancers until we found ourselves in the middle. We started dancing wildly while the audience cheered so enthusiastically it felt like they were more interested in us than Arafat. Then, to my surprise, Arafat's guards pushed through the circle and brought the great man, our new leader, into our circle. I stopped quickly, Ahmed only seconds behind me, watching him cautiously. But then we realised that he was laughing and suddenly he started dancing too. There were more cheers and shouts from the crowds while I showed off some complicated steps. Over two hundred thousand people were dancing and laughing, with us in the middle, dancing with Arafat. He held our hands and more people joined an inner circle until he walked back to his podium and started orating:

> "I had many dreams about this day. I lived my life for it. Whenever I was sad or scared of the future, I thought of this day. Today, we celebrate together. Not because of me, but because of the hope that our country now has. My friends, my heroes, my leaders; it is your sacrifice that has brought light to this day. It is your prayers and determination for the future that has led us here. Today we will start building our country. Together, we will make a future for our children. Together we will wash away the tears, we will shout for Palestine and the people who are watching us: "*Bilrouh! Bildam! Nafdeek Ya Filisteen*! With our souls and blood we will sacrifice for you Palestine!"

I shouted as loud as the rest thinking of all my sacrifices, a boy growing up without his father but somehow ending up a traitor, then a hero who risked his life in the battlefield. Even after the whole thing was finished and we headed home, I kept shouting with Ahmed and people joined us on the route home. We were not boys any more, we were suddenly born again that moment, new adults who have been scarred by occupation.

The whole week was full of excitement. We watched Arafat on TV visit different areas and forming the first Palestinian National Authority. It was also the first week that we were allowed to go out at night, as there were no soldiers to stop us. After it got dark people took everything outside. Their TVs, their games, even their cooking; they did everything in the street, enjoying their new-found freedom. They were thrilled at the idea of staying in the streets until morning. I got to know more people in our street this way, and spent time playing cards with neighbours and smoking shisha, which Mother was not at all happy about.

I began to understand why people wanted the peace agreement so much. I started enjoying it too. There were more weddings in the streets, big lunches and people coming and going at all hours. It felt like the country was alive again. Life was different in the few months following Arafat's arrival. By the time I got to high school, both Ahmed and I had made our minds up as to what we wanted to study at university and had already started to plan our future. I wanted to study English literature, keen to be able to speak another language and inspired by the tourists who now flooded into Gaza.

By the time I was sixteen, I had already learned some English. Ahmed wanted to study business so he could make some money and change his situation. Both of us studied hard at school, inspired by our new focus of getting into university and what that could lead us to. The search for Father became less important. Occasionally, Ahmed and I would discuss it, but I would quickly change the subject. Enough harm had been done. I was finally free and had a chance of a good future. I did not want to end up in trouble again. Not when I was doing so well.

Three years after Arafat had arrived, much had changed in the Gaza Strip. Investment from the Gulf was booming, tourists flooded the tiny Strip. I did not understand why people wanted to come and visit, thinking of it as having nothing except for a single beach. The streets were now paved much better and we had public parks and funfairs; things that had been completely foreign to us before. In the three years following Arafat's arrival, I felt like I had moved to a different country. Almost every week there was something new to discover. The trip from Jabalia to Gaza City was much easier now that the roads were fixed, and it became much cheaper with so many cars on the road. It was great to see Palestinians policing our streets.

I landed my first job during my final year of high school in 1997. I was sixteen, tall for my age and already using too much hair gel. Thanks to my training with the resistance, my body was lean and slightly muscular, making me look more like a twenty-five-year-old, than a teenager.

Then one morning Issam, the Fatah Party Youth Movement's regional manager, knocked on my door and asked me if I would be interested in working for the movement. Issam was very tall, with a long thin moustache and very small eyes and a bit of facial hair. He explained that he had heard about my participation in the resistance and that he would like me to work as a coordinator to recruit new members to the party, now that we were in times of peace. The pay was 150 Shekels a month plus benefits; such as help with schoolbooks and uniforms. I did not want to ask where he had heard about my history with the resistance, instead accepting his offer without any hesitation. A month later I was a political activist, leading the Fatah Society at school and working hard to get as many new members as possible. I roamed the Jabalia Camp, knocking on people's doors and talking to them about the advantages of joining the party.

I managed to recruit Ahmed who was hesitant at first, but then got into it as I explained my plans about what we could do with the money. There was now a 'safe passage' established between Gaza and the West Bank that people could use providing they went through extensive Israeli security checks. Our dreams became focused on how much money we could save in order to use that path to get to see another part of our country that we had never been to.

We became inseparable again, going around the camp together and talking to parents to convince them to make their children join our mission. I enjoyed spending time with Ahmed without having to worry about checkpoints or curfew. Mother let me get on with it and rarely interfered. I started staying at Ahmed's house even more often than before. Sometimes, Ahmed would leave the house early and Soumaya and I would have breakfast together before she left for university. By the time I finished high school in 1998, she was in her third year studying for a Bachelors in Arabic Literature at Al-Azhar University. I enjoyed our conversations and became more obsessed about staying over so we could get to speak in the morning when Ahmed was out. She seemed so delicate and beautiful. She spoke to me about university life, and how some classes were of mixed sex. I longed for when it would be my turn to go to university. I sometimes fantasized about having a coffee with her in the university café that she seemed to like so much, or us walking together to the beach, laughing and talking. I wanted to know how she felt about me.

12

In 1998, I officially joined the English department at Al-Azhar University in Gaza City. I cut my hair very short, wore sunglasses every day and paid more attention to how attractive I was than to my studies. The university was full of pretty girls and I never tired of noticing them. Ahmed let his hair grow, almost reaching his shoulders. He also left his facial hair go wild, which made him look like a young artist.

I was amazed to see so many students from different regions of the Strip. A lot of people from my high school class went to study at Birzeit University in the West Bank. More people came to visit Gaza and to spend time at the beach, as the West Bank had no access to the coast. West Bank girls were exotic beauties to me and I spent a lot of time on the beach trying to chat them up. The truth was that by the time I reached university and met all sorts of different people and beautiful girls, my desire to speak to Soumaya had lessened considerably. I still thought she was attractive, but not only was I distracted by this new page in my life, the fear of upsetting Ahmed stopped me from hanging out with her too much. She apparently noticed this, and one day at university decided to come up to me and talk about it

"Hey, Omar," she shouted from a distance.

"*Salam*, Soumaya, *keef Halek*?" I asked with a big smile.

"Good, you? I haven't seen you around in a while. Is everything all right between you and Ahmed?"

"Yes, yes of course."

"Why don't you come over anymore then?"

"Oh, university, you know. It is so busy and… I have a new job. I will be training to join the Preventive Security Forces."

"What? Are you out of your mind? Those people are nasty."

"Well, I have to earn money somehow and I have to pay my fees. Mother and Uncle said that they could not afford it. Why are they nasty? They are a national security force that could help us establish our free country."

She did not answer, but smiled and turned away. Whenever I went to see Ahmed over the following months, she avoided coming into the room and always made excuses and went out whenever she heard my voice in the house.

The job offer became official in December 1998. Issam asked if I was interested in working for the Preventive Security Forces under his command. He had become a Major and said that due to my gallant service to the national cause he would hire me as an Officer Cadet for $250 a month, which was too large a sum to turn down. I took great pleasure in the idea of funding my own studies and not having to rely on Mother or Uncle. In addition to paying off my fees, I would easily afford to buy the expensive English novels that our teachers demanded we read.

Mother was supportive of my education but wished I had studied something 'more practical'. In her opinion, there were no prospects for English literature graduates in Gaza. I did not really care. I was interested in letters, words and symbolism. When I read a book, I escaped into romantic notions and imaginary worlds; somewhere I could be a completely different person, for as long as I wanted. We argued about it when I first registered, but in the end she had to give in. There was no way I would change my mind.

Our relationship was changing as I entered my second year of university. She was more reliant on me as her health deteriorated. The beautiful, tall body she once had had started gaining weight. She became diabetic. She started to nag me to find someone to get married to so the future daughter-in-law could help with the housework. While I managed to prepare delicious meals with the cooking skills I had learned from my months living with Abu Hammad, she still complained that they were never like hers. This was probably true, but the reality was that I enjoyed looking after her. As we both grew up, our roles changed. I became the carer. I was able to understand her needs better as if she was my own child, but the scary thing was I could almost see that there was a big secret she was hiding from me. Every time I looked deep into her tired eyes, she would look away as if I was questioning her. I often caught her staring at me as I prepared a meal or did some tidying up. There was some uneasy tension between us, almost like she was my own prisoner waiting to confess something. Every morning I would wake up early and clean while she was still asleep. I would then go to the market and do the shopping, before changing into my newly acquired green military suit, heading to university before going to work in the evening. Issam was understanding and allowed me to complete my studies at the university.

"We need educated officers, not soldiers," he would say whenever I apologised for being late after classes. It helped that I excelled in training due to my experience of using guns and my martial art skills. Mother enjoyed watching me come home every evening dressed in my uniform. I often wished that Father were with us. We could have discussed things at the dinner table or smoked shisha and played some backgammon, while I told him about the new Palestinian Authority and my hopes for peace. His absence was exacerbated by Mother's illness. After exchanging pleasantries when coming home, I would head straight to her room and clean it. She was tired and couldn't move easily. She was no longer interested in going to doctors or even leaving the house.

She was decaying slowly and I knew that I wouldn't have her for much longer.

Uncle was trying to help by sending his children to do some shopping for us. He also insisted on paying, which hurt my pride. We hadn't talked very much since the day I returned from the resistance. If we hadn't been blood relations, we would have probably become complete strangers. Whenever I did see him though, my mind would travel back to the mission to find Father.

One Wednesday morning, as Ahmed and I skipped a lecture and headed down to the beach instead, life suddenly became beautiful again. We were complaining about our lecturers and I was filling Ahmed in on the latest news from work when I saw her. She was sitting on the beach with another guy who was doing his best to speak English. Being a rather arrogant man by now, I walked straight over and introduced myself.

"Omar. Pleased to meet you," I said in my best English accent. Ahmed continued to walk on the beach laughing at what he foresaw as an embarrassing situation.

"Can I help you?" she asked brusquely.

"Oh I thought you needed help, so I came…"

"What makes you think that? He's been trying to help me all day, every minute someone is trying to help me. I don't need any help."

She glared at the greasy-looking thin guy with broken teeth sitting next to her.

"Wow, easy. I am sorry to bother you, I just thought… Never mind. I must get back to my friend."

I ran back as fast as I could as Ahmed burst out laughing. My face burned with embarrassment and I punched him on the shoulder to make him stop.

He continued to laugh all the way back to the university.

In addition to the many people who came to Gaza with the Palestinian Authority, there were people who came from around the world either for political tourism or because they thought they could do something to 'help'. Most of them would stay for six months and most likely miss having simple pleasures like their cereal in the morning, leaving again as soon as possible. It was relatively easy for Europeans and Americans to come through the Erez Crossing and stay in Tel Aviv for a few days before coming to Gaza with bright ideas. The locals hated political tourists and dubbed them as the 'neo-orientalists'. I had never agreed with that until the day that brown-haired girl humiliated me on the beach in front of Ahmed. Even if she had been harassed by other guys that was not an excuse to be so abrupt with me.

One Friday morning, I went to pick up Mother's medicine from the UNRWA's Medical Practice and to my surprise, I saw the girl there. She was standing next to the Women's Voluntary Office, where women from the Jabalia Camp would volunteer to go around to people's houses and help out with the daily upkeep of the house. They only went to families who had a family member who had been badly injured or disabled during the *Intifada*. The dark brown hair stood out among the sea of white headscarves. I tried to ignore her, but I failed miserably. She was speaking to a woman who was using a lot of body language to communicate with her. Had it not been for her previous rudeness I would have offered to translate, as the poor woman looked old and tired. I saw her wipe tears off her eyes a couple of times.

In the end it was the foreign girl who approached me. In my terror, I clenched my suddenly sweaty fists and tried to ignore her.

"Hello, Captain," she said with a big smile on her face, almost as if she was mocking me.

"Sorry, are you talking to me?"

"Yes, you. The captain with the military suit. We met on the beach yesterday, remember?"

"You must have the wrong person, sorry." I looked away pretending to watch the queue. I was still angry with her.

"No, it's you. I remember faces very well. Look, I am sorry about yesterday. I had been followed all day and I was tired. Anyway, what are you doing here?"

"Waiting to see a film."

The smile on her thick lips made me smile too. Her hair was straight today. She was wearing dark green small egg-shaped earrings. I noticed her round cheeks pierced by dimples when she smiled. The white V-neck cotton top tucked into her tight blue jeans made her look exotic. Things were much more relaxed in Gaza then; many women went out without a headscarf. In fact, because a lot of Palestinian officials had arrived in Gaza from countries such as Lebanon, Syria or Jordan, a mix of attitudes towards conservatism was translated into a variety of dress codes in the streets.

"OK, chin up, Omar, I was in a bad mood yesterday. I am Zoe by the way."

She stretched her hand to shake mine. I hesitated, not knowing what to do. It felt like the entire room was watching. The pause was awkward, her smile started to disappear, but thankfully I snapped out of my daze and took her hand. The big smile on her red lips returned.

"So, you are not feeling well?" There was genuine concern in her voice.

"My mother isn't." I was trying hard not to stare at her breasts, my body temperature rising uncomfortably.

"I see."

"What brings you to this dump?"

She couldn't ignore the cynicism in my voice.

"This is a beautiful place, Omar. I know what you mean though; it can be rough to live here. I came to help out a little. I was studying conflict resolution and decided to take a year out after my second year and come here. It's my second month now."

"Interesting. I can only hope you find us interesting enough for your studies."

"It is not like that." Her eyes flashed angrily. "I did not say I was here for my studies. I said I took a year out. I am not here to study anyone. I am volunteering with local organisations. Sometimes I teach a bit of English. That's the only thing English people can do sometimes."

"You have an impressive amount of anger, Zoe."

We both laughed at that, diffusing the tension immediately. My turn at the pharmacy counter came and as I walked to it I looked back and smiled at Zoe. After I finished, I arranged to meet her for coffee in Gaza City the next day. It could not come soon enough.

That next morning it rained heavily, forcing me to dash back inside for my coat. Zoe was already waiting for me at the Daleice Café next to El-Shifa Hospital, wearing a green shirt, same tight blue jeans and a light grey cardigan.

"Are you not cold?"

She scoffed. "You call this cold? Seventeen degrees in February? Come to London if you want to experience some miserable weather."

"Let me just have a coffee first, then we'll go."

The waiter interrupted our chat to take our orders.

"You are full of yourself, Omar."

I ignored her comment. "Is that where you come from then, London?"

"Yes, although I was born in a small village in Surrey. We lived there for a while before moving to London. How come you are in the Security Forces?"

"What do you mean, how come?"

"Bit young, aren't you?"

"I have connections. Besides I am eighteen years old now – a full-grown man according to many international laws. How old are you anyway?"

"Two things you never ask a woman; her weight and her age," she smiled.

"Age means nothing. It is the experiences that you go through that add years to your life."

There was an uncomfortable pause as we sat there. Painful memories briefly resurfaced: Of being shot, of being abused by Uri, of Mother crying, of Father's picture.

"Are you OK?" she finally asked.

"Yes. Yes, fine. Do you fancy taking a walk to the beach?"

"Don't you have classes to attend?"

"Yes but forget about them, who cares? I am smart enough anyway."

"And you're also cocky."

"I am sorry!"

"Omar, I'm only teasing you."

We walked along the beach, sharing things about our lives. At first I was careful about what I shared with her. I certainly did not tell her about Uri. But I was more interested in hearing about her. I had been told that English people didn't open up easily, if at all. But I was surprised to find that Zoe seemed perfectly at ease with being open with me.

Zoe's parents were both doctors who had had to move whenever they were employed at a different hospital. When she was twelve, her father, William Abbot, a very successful surgeon, was offered a place at the hospital at University College, London, and her mother, Lindsey, was posted to the hospital in Newcastle in the north of England. Zoe moved to London with her father and lived with him, her mother visiting when she could. Over time, however, her parents' relationship began to deteriorate. Over breakfast one morning, William told his daughter that they were getting divorced. Zoe cried all the way to school.

As time passed, she got used to it and enjoyed going up north to visit her mother. It was a good escape from London's crowded streets. As she was travelling back one day from Newcastle to London, she saw an article in a copy of *The Guardian* left on the train about possible peace talks between the Israelis and the Palestinians.

"From then on, it was a slippery slope. I read lots of books and articles, researching the whole thing. Eventually I thought the best way to understand it would be to just go."

"And you picked Gaza? Why not the West Bank? It would have been much easier for you, no?"

"Always go off the deep end, my friend," she laughed.

We became very good friends. We met each other as often as we could, between my classes, work and looking after Mother. She also had a busy schedule and had to travel a lot to different parts of the Gaza Strip. She would tell me where she was and what she was up to and about all the people she met and I always looked forward to hearing about her adventures.

One day in late March 1999, Zoe was coming back from a trip to Khan Younis. She texted to invite me for a drink on the beach – which I accepted happily. She looked very tired when she arrived. We talked about what we had been doing and a little politics until Zoe admitted she was tired and I offered to walk her home. We started walking over Sheikh Ijleen Beach, then through to Ansar, going around Arafat's compound and ended up outside a recently built, eight-storey building.

"This is where I live. Do you want to come up?"

I hesitated for a moment. "That would be nice."

The stairwell had wide, stone steps and I stared at them and the marble walls as we ascended, my heart pounding as we reached the top floor. She looked nervous too as she struggled to unlock the door. The one-bedroom apartment was relatively big with a decent-size living room and a separate kitchen. Zoe went straight to the kitchen to get me a can of diet coke without needing to ask what I wanted. "Your favourite drink, mister."

"What are you having?"

"Thought about making some lemonade."

It felt nice to be there with her. I could almost pretend that we lived here together; that this was some routine we had settled into. She made her drink in silence as I walked across the apartment to the window. Gaza was beautiful in springtime, when the sun baked the buildings and the sea would be tempting like a giant swimming pool. As I stared out, Zoe came from behind me and put her arms around my waist, startling me. She stepped back startled herself.

"Sorry," she mumbled, unable to meet my gaze. I smiled and moved closer, until our bodies touched. I stroked her hair, then placed my hand underneath her chin and lifted her beautiful face upwards. Her wide eyes were glowing and a little smile played across her lips. She was the most beautiful girl in the world. At that point, it did not matter that she came from a completely different world. My ego grew as I realised that she wanted me just as much as I wanted her.

For the first time in my life I saw myself as a man, through her eyes. A man she lusted for; my masculine ego was getting bigger. My history did not matter then, I was a man in the arms of someone who was waiting for me to make the next move, shy and electrified. She was my woman. I kissed her. It was the first time I had ever kissed a woman in my life. She shut her eyes as our lips met, so I did the same without really knowing why. I opened them a couple of times to make sure that I hadn't gotten carried away and that she wasn't angry, but her eyes were closed all the time. She kissed me back, her tongue touched mine and her teeth bit my lips. My whole body trembled. I had never imagined how amazing kissing would feel.

I wasn't sure what to do next, afraid to make the wrong move and spoil the moment. But to my surprise, Zoe started unbuttoning her shirt. My breathing was getting heavier while we were still kissing. It felt like there was nothing else in the world but us, just the two of us in a tiny apartment in Gaza City. I took her shirt off and she followed suit by taking off mine. She paused for a few seconds, looking at my bare skin and touching my slightly hairy chest with her fingertips.

She lifted my right arm and started kissing my elbow, letting her tongue wonder the curves of my muscles and then down again until she got to my hand and licked my fingers. I watched her, the sensation was far too exciting, my mind was going crazy. I carried her to the bedroom and threw her on the bed. I began taking my trousers off but she stopped me and sat up on her knees in her white bra and black skirt. She started to kiss my belly as I stood there in front of her, then pulled me hard, making me collapse on the mattress.

She was taking control, which was fortunate because I had never done this before. She took my belt off, quickly unbuttoning my trousers, pulling them down and throwing them on the floor. They broke something as they landed, making us both laugh. But as she started taking off my underwear, I suddenly jumped. The last time someone took my pants off, I had been standing in Uri's office.

She paused, "Are you OK?"

"Yes, sorry… I… Please let's carry on."

"You look uncomfortable. I don't want to push you."

"No, you are not forcing me. Please do not stop… I… I have never done this before."

I looked away embarrassed, but she gently took my face in her hands and lifted it to face her smile.

We lay there as the breeze made the white curtain dance. She continued to stroke my chest while I ran my fingertips over her body. But our moment of pleasure did not last long as my mobile started to ring. I rejected the call, but it rang again and I thought I had better answer it. It was Issam, asking me to get to the Tel El-Hawa Security Centre immediately, as there was an emergency. Zoe did not understand any Arabic, but noticed the worried look on my face.

"What's wrong?"

"My boss. He needs me at work right now."

"Are you sure it's not your other girlfriend?" she teased me.

"Other? Does this mean I have one already?"

She smiled shyly and turned her face away, embarrassed at the question.

"Why would I need another if I have a great one right here?" I kissed her on the forehead as I started to retrieve my clothes. She put on her bathrobe and made us some refreshing mint tea. We drank in silence, smiling at each other over our cups, both blissful.

"When will I see you again?"

"Let's have dinner after work."

13

When I finally got to work that afternoon, the Tel El-Hawa Centre was unbearably hot. There were about three hundred soldiers inside the walls of the main square. As I pushed my way through, others were getting their gear ready. Issam appeared on top of a platform and started talking on a microphone.

"*Bismallah wa Tahiat El-Watan*, in the name of God and homeland greetings to you. We have summoned you here today as we are facing a threat to our national security and the future sovereignty of our cause. There are some people who refuse to adhere to the negotiations and reach an agreement with the Israelis in order for peace to prevail. Not because they care about Palestine, but because they want the power for themselves and they want to hold this nation hostage. We in the Fatah Party have resisted and led the national resistance movement as you all know. Now our great leader Yasser Arafat is giving peace a chance and we should stand by him. We should give him all the support he needs in order for this to succeed and end decades of war and destruction between us and our neighbour."

I did not like the way he talked about the 'neighbours', as if he had given up on his right to historical Palestine.

"I know some of these people who were fighting with you before the Palestinian Authority arrived in Gaza." He caught my attention. "Back then, all parties adopted the resistance formula. Now Hamas has decided to disobey the national agreement and disrupt talks with suicide bombings in Israel, killing innocent civilians. We cannot allow them to do this. We cannot allow them to spoil the hope for peace. We must go out and arrest them all to make sure that we all speak with one voice."

The crowds started muttering after he finished, returning to cleaning and loading their guns, putting on riot gear, banging on shields and helmets. But I couldn't help think of Soumaya, as I finally understood why she thought Preventive Security people were awful. We were about to do the Israelis' dirty work for them, while they kept their settlements in Gaza, arrested and shot at anybody any time they wanted. This peace agreement was a joke. I was on my way to our Division Office when I heard Issam's voice.

"Omar, wait!" He started running towards me. My heart started pounding. After his speech, whatever he had to say to me could not be good.

"Omar, listen. I want you to lead the raid on the Jabalia Camp. You are from there and know it well."

My blood froze.

"Please, do not ask me do this. These are my neighbours. I cannot shoot at them."

"I am not asking you Omar, I am ordering you."

"Sir! Please!"

"Omar, you are promoted to Second Lieutenant."

The order was clear: To arrest all members of Hamas. But Hamas was still in its infancy as a party. It was mainly run from mosques, like the El-Khulafa Mosque in the Jabalia Camp. Arresting them meant that I had to invade that mosque I had prayed in all my life. It meant potentially arresting anyone who had a beard. It meant that anyone could be hurt along the way.

My unit was ready, waiting for my first order as Second Lieutenant. I pointed at a blue van for them to get into and then headed to get my gun, leaving my phone and wallet in my locker before I joined my men. Over the radio, I asked Issam for reinforcements, as the Jabalia Camp was a Hamas stronghold. He informed me that the Palestinian police had taken over El-Markaz and was ready for our arrival to support the operation. Our orders were to arrest anyone suspected of being a Hamas member and put them in El-Markaz until they were transferred to Tel El-Hawa.

There was no electricity when we arrived and, as it was a hot evening, most people were out on the street. The Major in charge of the police force there received me with a salute, even though I was technically his junior. Our Preventive Security Forces were of higher status than the police force and had the power to override their authority. I noticed that there was a cluster of young police officers in blue uniform to the side of the main entrance.

The operation was planned in the Major's office – Uri's former office. I remembered the first time I stepped inside that door as an innocent young boy searching for his father. That journey had turned me into a collaborator. The same thing would happen tonight after leaving this office. My neighbourhood would see me as responsible for arresting my own people. Instead of the weak, abused child, I was now the one who was about to order the abuse.

I gave the captains and police officers clear instructions on which streets to block and which areas to attack. The El-Khulafa Mosque was left to my forces to surround and carry out arrests, as none of the police captains were willing to risk their lives or their officers in the operation. We set out in the dark, right after the end of the evening prayer. I knew that the ordinary people would have prayed and returned home and only the Hamas leadership would remain in the mosque. When we got there, the lights were down. My instructions were not to fire unless absolutely necessary, and only to defend life, promising to shoot anyone who disobeyed that order. My glare told the soldiers I was serious. The silence shattered as we heard gunshots in the distance from El-Hawaja Street, where another unit was moving against two houses for Hamas leaders. Screams and sirens filled the air.

We waited around the nearby street corners. My plan was to arrest anyone who came out of the mosque, hopefully without firing a single shot. As we waited, hiding behind bins and broken trees, a silhouette appeared in the dark on the empty street.

They approached us slowly. My men loaded their guns and took aim, but I waved at them to lower their guns. I recognised the figure. Um Marwan.

I left my hiding place and ran to her. It was almost as if she had been expecting me. She stopped as soon as she saw me approach. She looked at me sadly, shaking her head slowly.

"Your father would be ashamed of you, Omar. You disgrace him."

Not even when she found out I was a collaborator did Um Marwan say such a thing to me. Was it because I was only a boy then? Had she hoped that I would change? Was that why she had never talked to me like this before?

Suddenly I heard gunshots close to us. I grabbed her, keeping her head down as I moved her to the corner, telling her to wait for me. I turned back to watch the battle unravel, some of my men already firing back while others getting ready to enter the mosque. I had to stop them before they committed a massacre.

I ran towards them, yelling at them to hold their fire and retreat. As they returned to their places, confusion reigned again as more shots were fired. I looked up to my left and saw a masked man at the window of one of the nearby houses, shooting at us with his pistol. I ordered the men to retreat to the van before kicking down the door in my hunt for the gunman. In one room, lit by a small candle, I discovered a frightened old woman sitting there. She had her eyes closed and her ears covered against the noise.

The gunman did not notice me until I was right behind him, my gun at his head.

"Drop it or I will blow your head off!" I shouted. He did not move. I hardened my voice. "I swear I will."

A few seconds later he dropped the gun.

"Lean against the wall."

I searched his body for more weapons before kneeling down to pick up the gun. "Turn around," I ordered, then wished I had not. I would recognise those eyes anywhere, having spent months trying to read them. Abu Hammad stood there, hands on his head, completely at my mercy.

"Abu Hammad, what are you doing here?"

"What you refused to do. Resisting, my little friend."

"How is this resisting?"

"By refusing to be Israel's henchmen .Why are you arresting us?"

"For the awful stuff you do. For disrupting the peace process."

"What peace are you talking about, you fool? Do you know how many people they've killed since you and your men became the so-called Palestinian Authority? Do you know how many have been arrested? There is no peace. These negotiations were designed to give Israel more time to kill us and uproot us from this land, with people like you policing it. We will not be treated as fools. We will not be collaborators to this aggression."

"Do not call me a collaborator. You know my story. You are the last one I would have expected to hear this from."

"Yes, I know your history. I know you too well. You are a coward, that is what you are. You want to save your skin and climb the power ladder. But I will not go anywhere with you. You will have to kill me here. I will not be put in a Palestinian prison. We are brothers, one people. We are meant to be together, not arrest and kill each other."

I raised my gun to his face and put my finger on the trigger. I stared at him, remembering how he was the person who had taught me to use a wretched gun in the first place. Sweat poured down my forehead as I cursed at my indecision. This man was my friend. He had been my only companion for months and now here I was, holding a gun to his face. He looked at me in defiance, daring me to shoot him. He was braver than I ever was, or could be.

I lowered my gun.

"Go, Abu Hammad. Go before anyone else comes." He stared at me. "I said go. GO!"

He started moving slowly towards the door, my gun pointing at the floor. At the door, he stopped and turned round to face me again. His hands reached to his *kufiyyah* that was wrapped around his face. He untied one end and let the mask fall to his shoulders. It was the first time I ever saw his face. I was shocked to see how young he looked. Unlike what I had imagined, Abu Hammad did not have a beard or a moustache, but was completely clean-shaven. He had ginger hair and dark brown eyes, both seeming to gleam in the moonlight. His thin lips smiled at me.

He nodded at me in farewell and I returned the gesture. I listened as he descended the stairs, waiting until I knew for sure he was gone, before leaving myself. I heard a floorboard creak as Abu Hammad stopped.

"Omar," he called back up to me, "one more thing. Your father is alive in one of the prisons in Israel. Ask your uncle. He knows everything."

I ran to the top of the stairs, but he had already disappeared. I shouted back at him and was tempted to send my men after him. But then he would get arrested. Once again, I had to choose between arresting an innocent person or miss knowing more about Father. Uri's threats came flashing back to my mind, reminding me of that cursed day when I left the piece of paper for his soldiers and thus became a traitor. I let go of all those memories as I fell down on my knees at the bottom of the stairs. I was suddenly tired of feeling like everyone knew about Father except me. Why did it feel like everyone I knew was hiding something from me?

Back out in the streets, I realised Um Marwan was gone too. Gunshots were being fired from inside the mosque. My men had disobeyed my orders, arresting as many people as they could and opening fire on the mosque. I went inside as quickly as possible and took charge of the operation once again, ordering my men to take the prisoners outside. I wandered through the empty hall of the mosque, reeling at all the destruction around me. I thought about Abu Hammad calling me a collaborator. He was right. Before, I would pass names of resistance members to the Israelis and they would handle the dirty work. Now, I was the one doing the arresting and killing, without having to even rely on a piece of paper with a name scribbled down. Was this what Soumaya tried to warn me about the Preventive Security Forces all those years ago? Was this why she had stopped talking to me?

When I got back to the office around midnight, I was greeted with applause from Issam, who believed I had planned and executed a good operation. The first thing I had on my mind was the dinner I had missed with Zoe. I looked at my mobile and saw four missed calls from her. It was too late to call now and there was no energy left in me to make excuses, so I decided to postpone calling until tomorrow. I sat there among all the tired officers who were chatting and showing off. I finally let my mind turn to Father. I always knew it in my heart, but to have Abu Hammad confirm he was alive was a revelation. I was angry that he had had all those months to tell me, but perhaps he had not wanted to distract me from my work in the resistance. Maybe he thought I did not want to know, after all I had been through. Perhaps this was his way of thanking me for letting him go.

So Uncle knew everything, didn't he? Did he know where Father was and had not told me? My relief and exhaustion suddenly gave way to a burst of anger. I wanted to find Uncle and put a gun to his head. I would demand that he tell me everything, and shoot him if he refused.

I called Ahmed at 1am that morning, and he was relieved to hear from me after hearing all the gunfire. I told him everything that had happened. When I was done, he suggested we meet after university the next day and try to figure out my next step.

We were dismissed at the break of day. I went straight to Zoe's apartment, went upstairs and knocked on the door. She appeared wearing a nightgown, still half-asleep. "What are you doing here?"

"Sorry, I need to rest. I cannot bear going home."

I told her everything, leaving out the part about Abu Hammad, as I still had not told her the entire truth about Father.

"Why are you doing this, Omar?"

"Doing what?"

"Arresting your own people."

"Those were the orders, I can't disobey."

"You should quit the Palestinian Authority as soon as possible. It has done nothing but turn people against each other. Who are you doing this for, and at what price? Next you might have to arrest your own mother."

I looked at her surprised, not knowing how to respond to that. I thought of Um Marwan and how she looked down on me when she saw me with my gun, trying to arrest our neighbours.

"What brought you to Gaza, Zoe?"

"I told you before. I watched all the news about the conflict here and wanted to see it for myself, I wanted to help. Maybe it is too naïve of me to think that I could, but I'm here. I am trying my best to see how I can help."

"I am also trying to help. In my own way. Maybe if we have peace for just a few years, maybe my people will relax into it and they will see that it is actually more beautiful than fighting."

"But they don't have any choice. The Israelis are imposing heavy sanctions, arresting, killing people whenever they want to."

"Stop lecturing me, Zoe. Don't tell me about how much we suffer. I have gone through it most of my life."

I was breathing heavily trying to keep myself calm.

"Well, if you have suffered so much why are you making others suffer too?"

"That is so typical of you British people. You were the cause of this problem. So please, do not lecture me about my country and its sufferings. Your people have done enough."

I was angry with everything around me. Angry for being labelled every time I tried to do something. Angry for being accused of collaboration when I genuinely thought that giving peace talks a chance would work. I was frustrated because my father was alive somewhere and I could not reach him. I was furious because my uncle had betrayed me. I felt like going back to the office, pulling my gun and shooting myself, killing my anger once and for all. Instead I left. I headed home to see Mother.

She was just waking up, coughing profusely as she walked through the corridor from her room towards the living room where I had started tidying up. The room was a complete mess; she had left a big woolly blanket on the floor, a few empty bottles of Coke scattered around, along with empty packets of crisps.

She managed to say 'good morning' in between her coughs. She washed her face at the sink by the door. Her white bathrobe was beginning to look grey. It upset me to see her so frail.

"Have you taken your medicine?" I was upset by the state she was in.

"No, I do not need it."

'Mother, you should. You will make yourself worse."

"Don't tell me what to do, I can look after myself perfectly well."

I did not look at her as I continued tidying up. "Mum, where is Father?"

She coughed again, a terrible hacking sound, while she grabbed a towel and dried herself, as if trying to gain more time to think of the answer.

"How many times do I need to tell you the same story? You are a man now, Omar. You have to accept these things and let them go."

"The trouble is, Mother, the story you told me is not true and I am asking you now because I will find out myself, and I will not be happy then."

"Are you threatening me?" She was staring at me defiantly as if daring me to try. I stared at her, shocked that she would consider anything I said a threat to her.

"Of course not, but I have the right to know where Father is. All I am asking is for you to tell me the truth."

"I told you the truth several times. If you do not believe it then that is entirely your problem, but I have nothing else to say."

There was no point in trying again with her, she was determined as ever to give me the usual version, the same script she had prepared. Her eyes were accusatory, as if I was the one who was being unreasonable. The house had become so claustrophobic that I had to get out. I took a taxi from the Jabalia Camp to Gaza City and then changed to another to get to my university. I had no lectures that morning, but I preferred to go to the library and read for a bit. My brain was about to explode with the morning's arguments with Zoe and Mother. I was feeling sorry for myself, annoyed about how everything seemed shaped by politics. I had gone from being in a relationship to being single in one night. Restless, I went to the university library and found a battered copy of *Kalila Wa Dimna*, and spent the morning reading.

Once upon a time, there was a beautiful city surrounded by two rivers that made it a trading centre for merchants that came from far afield. Because of the rivers, the people were able to go out and sell their goods easily and they became rich and prosperous. The people loved their cats, almost everyone owning one as a pet. Now there was a big and powerful mouse that was king of all the mice in the city. He had three wazirs, ministers, whom he called for one day.

"I need your advice on an urgent matter. We have lived in this city for a long time, in the very tunnels that our forefathers have built for us. This is a prosperous place and there is plenty for us to live on. However, this happiness is always threatened by our fear of cats and, although we have done very well, I would like to seek your advice on how to get rid of them and live in more peace than past generations."

"It's simple," the first wazir said as everyone turned towards him. "What we need to do is find small bells that we can hang on the cats' necks at night, so that we can hear them when they are coming and we can run and hide quickly. This way, there will be no surprises and more lives could be saved."

"What do you think of this suggestion?" the King of mice asked the second wazir.

"I think it's stupid. The cats will still be there and we will still have to rely on our quick legs to escape. We will be afraid of bells and cats for the rest of our lives. I have a better plan. We should all leave the city for a year, so the people believe there are no mice anymore. They will then realize that, since there are no mice around, there is also no need for cats to hunt them down. In a month or two they will understand that the cats have no real use and that they are only eating their food, so the people will kick them out to save money and the cats will scatter and fight and kill each other over the remaining food on the street. We can go back when most cats will have deserted the city in search of a new place."

"Interesting," said the King, before turning to the third advisor: "what do you think, most wise wazir?"

"It's too risky. We don't know how long this whole process will take and the people are fond of their cats, they would not just banish them for eating their food. What we need to do is hatch a plan to make people hate their cats. Your majesty should order all the mice to dig one big tunnel into the house of the richest man in the city. We

should not eat any of the man's food, but instead tear his clothes. When he suspects the mice of being responsible for this, he will get another cat to help his own with the hunt. We will then start tearing his bed sheets. He will then think that he needs another cat and when he gets one, we will start tearing the furniture.

"As we step up our assault, the man will suspect that the increased number of cats was the reason for his clothes and furniture being ripped. Therefore, he will decide to experiment and get rid of one cat. We will then decrease our attacks. He will try again and we will do the same until he gets rid of the final cat, at which point we will stop completely. The man will then run to the neighbours and inform them of his discovery. As a result everyone will start getting rid of their cats, to prevent the same from happening."

The King thought long and hard about his choices and in the end decided to build the tunnel, as advised by the third wazir. The mice worked hard for a whole year to construct their tunnel, but the goal was achieved earlier than hoped for, and within a month the people of the city began to hate their cats. If they noticed that someone's jacket had been torn or a bit of food had been eaten, they swore that a cat must have done it. If a man or a woman got ill they would blame the cursed cats. Within three months the city was cleansed of all cats, while the mice lived happily in the city ever after.

I closed the book and leaned against the wall, wondering whether I was the mouse who drove the cats away last night. Whoever thought of the Oslo agreement must have had the same mind as the third wazir.

14

I had just finished a falafel sandwich at the university café and was about to start my tea, when Ahmed came up from behind and threw a newspaper on the table. I looked at him in shock, but he pointed at a small section at the bottom of the front page of the *El-Ayyam* newspaper, which he had already circled with a red pen.

El-Ayyam Newspaper, Issue 256, 17 May 1999.

by Ruba El-Helou

In a new development, police sources have confirmed the arrest of Mr. Khayyam El-Farra, the infamous solicitor who has been accused of deceiving people into selling their properties before the Palestinian Authority arrived in Gaza. Sources close to top officials in the Ministry of Interior have confirmed that the police now have concrete evidence of unlawful transactions, which the solicitor undertook on behalf of American Jews wishing to buy properties. After the deportation of nearly 800,000 Palestinians, Israel declared Palestinian homes as State property and has since populated them with new Jewish immigrants. Refugees have always held on to their right of return and kept legal documents and keys to their properties. However, it is believed that Mr. El-Farra was contacted by an American Jewish organisation and received large sums of money in order to get people to hand their legal documents to this organisation.

Although there hasn't been any change since the tragedy started and our people have been killed and deported, Police are calling on people to come forward if they have had any dealings with this man. It's also widely believed that Mr. El-Farra was a spy for the Israeli occupying forces during their time in Gaza and used to blackmail those who refused to hand over their papers. Some of them ended up in prison, others were even deported from Gaza and very few people know their whereabouts. We will update you on the developments as they come to us.

I closed the paper and looked at Ahmed who was completely apprehensive.

"So, Father could've tried to sell the house and this man tricked him or even put him in prison?" I asked, hoping Ahmed would agree with me and we would finally resolve the issue.

"That could be the case. We have to investigate before we do anything."

"But what about what Abu Hammad said, that Uncle knew everything?"

"He probably does, but without finding more information ourselves we will never get anything out of him. You will just hear the same story over and over again."

I thought about my argument with Mother that morning.

"You will need to try and interview that solicitor and get the truth out of him. Don't rely on news articles. You need to speak to him directly and ask him about your father. Use your connections at work."

I looked at my friend, grateful for his unwavering support. We drank tea together and continued hatching our plan. He was going to try and get some more information from Um Marwan. Ahmed believed that she too had not told me the whole truth, perhaps because she was too close to me or afraid of my mother and uncle. I remembered suddenly how Um Marwan often referred to our house as 'cursed' and refused to come in. She never got on with Mother either.

Ahmed set out to see her after he was done with classes and I returned to work. Issam was waiting, eager to talk more about what had happened last night and to congratulate me. As I walked through the main entrance of Tel El-Hawa, I could hear the tortured screams of those I had arrested the night before. Issam seemed to ignore it, as if it was noise coming from a construction site, an inevitable disruption to the business. His face was full of energy, as if he had just liberated Jerusalem and returned the whole of Palestine to her rightful owners.

"Why are we torturing them, Issam?" I spoke slowly but loud enough for him to realise that I was not happy.

"These are the orders; we need to get more information."

"About what?"

"Well, other people involved, attacks planned for the future," he said matter-of-factly.

"But these people are not fighting us; they are fighting the Israelis. Why are we making our own people hate them as if they were the ones who committed the crimes against us?"

"If they were in our position they would have probably shot us by now. They are lucky they are still alive."

"They might shoot us later, but it will be because of what we are doing to them today."

Issam looked at me in surprise, no doubt wondering where my sympathy was coming from. I did not agree with them, but I did not agree with the way we were torturing them. Hearing them being slapped and dragged across their cells reminded me of the first time I went to El-Markaz and heard how the Israelis were torturing our people. I wondered what the difference was between them and us. This damn peace agreement: Security for Israel with Palestinian illusion of self-control. The satisfaction stemming from the 'freedom' we had been given as part of the Oslo agreement was beginning to fade.

Hope was temporarily revived when Yasser Arafat and Ehud Barak, the Israeli prime minister, started the final stage of peace talks that could bring the Palestinian state to life. But when both leaders came back home without agreeing on anything, people became depressed, knowing that their circumstances were not going to change any time soon. Every day when I went home from university, I saw more and more people sitting on the side of the road with grim looks on their faces. Slowly, I started to see that the situation would explode one day and when it did, it was going to become worse than it had ever been.

I did not want to go home that evening, instead I went to the Beach Hotel in Gaza City to have dinner and smoke shisha. To my surprise, I saw Zoe sitting on her own, eating a plate of Fattoush salad. I headed straight to her table. She looked at me and smiled.

"I thought I wasn't going to see you again."

"I thought you didn't want to see me again."

We both smiled as I said this. I apologised for my behaviour earlier and finally explained what I had been going through.

I told her about my missing Father for the first time and she listened in astonishment. I even confessed to her that I collaborated with the Israelis and, to my surprise, this did not make her hate me.

On the contrary, she felt overwhelmed to be trusted with my story. She gave me a hug and apologised in return for not understanding me better. We took a walk on the beach after we finished, holding hands. She held mine really tight as if trying to reassure me that things would change for the better. That she was there. For the first time in my life, I felt someone had finally understood all the abuse I had gone through. I had never dared to tell anyone my story of collaboration with the Israelis. Even Ahmed did not know. But Zoe knew how to let me trust her. She was there that evening, giving me the attention that I needed. No one had ever done that for me.

Ahmed continued to visit me in the hope that he would see Um Marwan and get more information out of her. She never really gave him anything, save for one thing. One day as Ahmed left my house on a cold evening in December 1999, he saw her sitting outside with an old twenty-litre olive oil can that she had made some holes in and inside she was burning some wood to keep herself warm. Ahmed went straight to her and started warming his hands above the small flames coming out. I could see both of them from the window and realised that I could hear them quite well, given that our two houses were close. I quickly pulled the blinds down and turned the light off, becoming invisible.

"How is Omar?" she asked as she rubbed the palms of her hands together to get more heat.

"He is well, a bit overworked in my opinion though. It is not easy to study, work and look after an ill mother. I often feel sorry for him."

"He shouldn't have taken that wretched work," she said, as she looked up towards Ahmed in anger.

"Well, he has to pay for his fees; he doesn't have anyone to support him. The allowance they get is barely enough for them to live on, never mind paying expensive university fees. Besides everyone is joining the Palestinian Authority, there might be a future there. I am considering it myself."

"Don't, Ahmed, please don't," she pleaded and there was sadness in her eyes. "Omar is already suffering so much. Please try to convince him to leave."

"You know, you seem more concerned about Omar than his mother. I worry for her too. I think she is abandoning herself to despair."

"Well, that Souad, she shouldn't be here in the first place."

"What?"

"Mustafa and Souad should never have married to start with."

"Why?"

"She brought so much misery to this happy family and to the whole neighbourhood."

"How?"

"Never mind, forget what I said."

She then got up and went inside the house as I rushed out and joined Ahmed, stretching my hands over the fire to get some heat. He looked at me with pride, as if confirming his conspiracy theory that Um Marwan knew more than she told us.

It took about three more months to track down the infamous solicitor and to get permission to see him in person. In March 2000, I went to Abu Khasra Prison in the middle of Gaza City and was told that he had been moved to El-Abbas Prison. I headed there quickly with my permission papers in hand. The officer in charge of his case was surprised to see me dressed up in my military uniform with the star on my shoulder, reflecting my Second Lieutenant rank. He stood up immediately and saluted. I was nineteen years old then with a very small, designer stubble beard. I showed him my papers and he took me to another office, where I waited for Khayyam to appear, handcuffed and dressed in a striped blue and white uniform. He had yellow teeth and one of them was missing. His olive skin looked pale as if he had not seen the sun for a long time.

"Sit down," I ordered, watching him nervously pulling a chair with his handcuffed hands before settling down.

"I am here to ask you a few questions about a case you managed towards the end of the seventies. Mr. Mustafa Ouda, my father, does the name ring a bell?" He did not answer my question and just stared at my uniform, inspecting the star carefully.

"Do you know him?" I asked him again, using a more authoritative voice.

"I refuse to speak without my lawyer present," he replied.

"Have it your way, but trust me, if this is the way you want to play it, I will ask for your transfer to Tel El-Hawa, to our Preventive Security headquarters. There, lawyers and human rights organisations don't dare enter and when they do, it is normally too late. It is your choice."

I could almost see his brain working, weighing his options.

"What do you want to know?"

"My uncle, Mr. Attiya Ouda, wrote to you about the property in Sanaida Street, Jabalia Camp, and you informed him that the matter was in your hands and that you had not received any further instructions from my father, Mr. Mustafa Ouda."

"I am sorry, I do not remember any of that."

"Well, try," I growled at him.

"Look, I am accused of betraying the entire nation by selling people's houses to Israelis. I am not aware of any charge against me about a house in a small scruffy camp somewhere in Gaza."

"So, did you only specialise in deceiving people to sell their houses? Why?"

"Well, they are never going to get their homes back anyway. Israel is not going anywhere, so they might as well receive money for them to help them in their poor conditions."

"Not because you wanted money for yourself?"

"I have done nothing wrong; I was clear with everyone. They were naïve enough to sell. I explained everything to them clearly. Anyway, who are you to come here asking questions in that tone? If you have anything against me, then bring it to court."

I had run out of patience, I stood up with fiery eyes. "I will return in two weeks with the order to transfer you to Tel El-Hawa in my hand. That, of course, will depend on whether your memory recovers beforehand. Now, you will go to your cell, squeeze that bald head of yours and try to remember everything."

I slammed the door behind me and ordered the policeman to take him back to his cell. I was confident that I could transfer him to our headquarters. With my position in the Preventive Security Forces, I could easily ask Issam for a favour and, if he did not agree, I could happily speak to my seniors about this case and get him under my watch.

But it took longer than I expected and it was not until the second *Intifada* that I managed to get him transferred to our centre. I went home straight away that day. Even though it was late March, there were lots of clouds in the sky, rain starting to drizzle. Mother was out when I arrived home, so it was easy to go back to the drawer and check the legal documents once again. The Turkish ownership paper, the key and all the other files were still there. I held them in my hands and stared at them for a long time, wondering whether Father had made a big mistake and had also been fooled by that awful man.

It scared me to think that Father might have been naïve enough to sell his original house in our homeland. We had a large black key with a big keyring at the end of it, but no door to open it with. A flattened house that was most likely occupied by someone else, or perhaps even transformed into a farm. But that key was our only hope that one day, after having endured this horrible life in a refugee camp, we might be able to return home.

15

It was the same moustached officer who checked Omar's Palestinian passport to make sure the exit stamp from Queen Alia Airport, Amman, was there. His moustache was almost dancing with glee on his two fat lips as he stared at Omar's face while flicking the pages without reading a word of it.

"Good boy, did we really have to do this to remind you that you are Palestinian? We are doing this for your own good, so you don't forget who you are and where you come from." His words were followed by a loud guffaw that made everyone in the queue edge forward to see what was happening.

"Where do I wait this time?" Omar was about to turn when another tall policeman came and led him through the immigration desk, then behind all the other officers and through a narrow corridor until they reached the exit door. They started descending long dirty steps; Omar could see two mice with the corner of his eyes. He knew exactly where he was going. He had been to that disgusting deportation room allocated for all Palestinian travellers before. They kept going down until the air around them became damp; he looked at his phone, relieved that it was nearing midnight but worried that the battery would run out any minute.

Another policeman, sitting on a short plastic grey chair, stood up and saluted Omar's bodyguard, who waved for the door to stay open. Many others were crowded behind the door and stepped back immediately as soon as Omar was pushed in. They stared at him for a bit and then went back to their business. Some stayed to ask him where he came from. As soon as he sat down, a couple of young men who were studying in Turkey started talking about the massacre of Shejaiya in the latest attacks and analysing the situation, wondering whether Hamas had actually captured an Israeli soldier or not. They were from the same area and had lost family members amongst the more than one hundred people killed when Israel flattened the neighbourhood entirely. Omar sat there listening to them, remembering the time when he had been shot as a boy. And then he recalled learning how to use a gun and becoming a hero. He thought about what could've happened to him, had he stayed in Gaza. Would he have been the one capturing an Israeli soldier?

The 3x3 room was full of at least 30 men and women, young children and babies. Some had been there for a week waiting for the moment the Rafah Border would open so they could be put on a bus accompanied by two soldiers and sent through the Sinai, on a seven-hour journey to Gaza.

To Omar's delight, everyone asserted that they were promised to be on the move in the morning, as there was news of a seventy-two-hour ceasefire between resistance movements and Israel. The border would open briefly for humanitarian relief to be let in. Omar couldn't wait to get out of the stinking basement room. It had not been washed for at least a month, he thought to himself. He sat down on the floor, back to the wall and watched people around him stare at him. He had at least eight hours before they would be on the move and seven more hours on the bus to get to the border. Hands shaking, panting, he was not sure whether he should carry on writing or not. How would Mustafa feel once he tells him everything? Should he carry on regardless?

But time went by quickly as he listened to the chatter of people analysing the latest Israeli assault on Gaza. Most of them agreed that it was a premeditated attack. Omar hadn't visited Gaza since 2011 and he missed sitting around his people chatting in Arabic and talking politics all the time, which was the main topic of discussion in Gaza when people visited each other. It was part of life almost like discussing the weather with everyone in England.

Before he knew it, an Egyptian officer walked through the door and started shouting in Arabic, announcing that they would be put on a bus to Rafah. He started reading out the names of travellers, asking them to form a queue outside the door. The news was that the ceasefire would take place at 8am on Friday, August the 1st and the border would open shortly after, at 10am. They were led back up the stairs by the officer in charge of the deportation operation, who held a blue flip chart and walked ahead, occasionally glancing back like a primary school teacher making sure the kids didn't stray. In the arrival hall, their bags were queued while they marched to pick them up before being stopped again to be searched, then form a queue again, then searched again before they exited the hall, then stopped again before they left the airport and searched again. Then they carried on to the car park and once the old Mercedes bus had arrived, they were searched one final time. The officer radioed two other army officers who brought everyone's passport in a plastic bag. They got on the bus, smiling, some even made the victory sign with their fingers. Omar, looked around at the cheering faces, asking himself why those people were so happy to willingly walk back into another prison.

The bus kept stopping on the way as the driver and the three officers wanted bribes from the passengers. They threatened that if the travellers didn't pay, they would turn back and put them in the same deportation room they came from. Everyone paid unwillingly. As they crossed the Suez Canal, Omar's phone beeped. Ahmed's name on his phone glared at him as the preview of the text message appeared on his screen:

"Everyone is fine el-hamdullah, *they are staying at Um Marwan's. I will go and see them once the shelling slows down a bit. It is too dangerous to leave now."*

The relief made Omar's eyes water as he leaned back on his seat. He then smiled a little smile as tears ran down his cheeks profusely. They were alive and that's what mattered, everything else then became just details. He texted Zoe immediately to let her know the good news and that he was still on his way to Gaza. He felt like standing up in the middle of bus and dancing like a maniac, but he feared offending others or making the officers angry.

By the time they got to the Egyptian side of Rafah, the mood had changed. As they were hurdled down the bus and taken to the departure area of the Egyptian side of the border, they heard on one of the officers' walkie-talkie that the ceasefire had been broken and that the border was shut. No one was allowed in or out of Gaza. Orders came through to take all travellers to a nearby police station given that the Palestinian side of the border was being struck. Omar heard the news on the bus radio that Israel was bombing Rafah, after claiming that Hamas had captured another of their soldiers. A mixture of jubilation and sadness overtook the faces of the travellers who knew that they had missed their chance of going into Gaza for the time being and that they might have to go back to the deportation room. Omar was pleased to know that he could get back to London if he chose to, unlike all of his poor fellow travellers. His British passport would warrant him a flight back to London. But he was very apprehensive, he hadn't come all this way to turn and go back.

They could hear the sound of Israeli bombs falling, shaking the small police room they sat in. There was no food or water, children were crying, others got their praying mats and started praying that God would stop this madness and allow them to get back to their families. The room was very hot, with no working fans, flies filling the place, roaming people's faces, landing on their cheeks. By evening, Hamas had already announced that they had not captured any soldier. Omar knew then that this was no more than an Israeli lie to allow them to continue their onslaught. The border wouldn't open for a while. They had no choice; they were all put back on the bus to be driven through the night back to the deportation room. An old man tried to run away from the Egyptian soldiers, who then started shooting in the air, making him freeze on the spot. When they got to him, they started beating him mercilessly. Omar stared through the bus window at this old man being beaten by young Egyptian officers feeling helpless to do anything about it. None of the other deportees dared move, they knew they would be in far greater trouble if they interfered. Omar wondered whether people in London would believe that such treatment existed, that people on that bus were being punished just for being Palestinians.

Even though he knew he wasn't getting into Gaza, he still took out his notebook to finish the story addressed to his son. After this trip, he felt that he might never be able to tell him of his shame in person; he might not be able to describe how helpless he was. He might never be able to look his son in the eye and tell him that he had nearly killed his uncle, that he himself was going to become like the Imam who killed his meerkat. Omar sat in the dark bus staring out of the window. He could see both Egyptian and Israeli watchtowers looking over Gaza. A big part of him was relieved that he was going back to London, to his wife and child and that he got the news he had wanted to hear, that everyone was still alive. But seeing and hearing the bombs falling on his home was like watching a car in a scrapyard, smashed and reduced to pieces before being sent for recycling. He didn't know when or if ever he will be able to visit again, and was sad that he couldn't bring that photo back to London either. His whole mission was ruined by the border closure. As the engine of the bus started, he took out his notebook and decided to carry on with the story of the cursed house, of betrayal, of love and a lost hope. The sound of the bombs reminded him of the beginning of the second Intifada *when everything fell to pieces again, when he knew that there was no hope left in that wretched Strip anymore.*

16

We all saw him on TV and knew that peace was over. Ariel Sharon, the Israeli defence minister was entering Al-Aqsa Mosque in Jerusalem. I did not understand what he was doing there.

It was September 2000 and he was surrounded by almost three thousand soldiers, all guarding him. The camera panned around to show Palestinians throwing their shoes at the soldiers who were pushing them inside the mosque. As the camera moved between the two scenes, more shoes flew and then the sound of bullets ripped through the air. The soldiers started shooting at people who had come for prayer. There were a lot of people running around like mad, some trying to enter the mosque to take cover from the bullets, others lying on the ground and dozens running between the soldiers and the entrance to the mosque. Ariel Sharon did not look concerned by what was happening; he continued to look ahead, ignoring what was happening to his left.

I knew then that it was about to start all over again. The news played it every hour, while many politicians gave their analysis of the situation. Most of them agreed that the troubles would disappear the next day, that people were simply reacting to the moment, and that everything would soon be forgotten. But I felt differently. I knew this was going to be a new *Intifada*.

Mother looked troubled but didn't speak about it at all.

Instead, she did a lot of tidying up that day, for the first time in ages. I knew she was keeping herself busy in order not to think. The next day there was more news. Six people had been killed in confrontations with the soldiers in the West Bank and three more joined them in the evening. We watched closely while Palestinian national TV played more patriotic songs than ever.

Gaza was still calm and nothing had changed, but the day after I could not get to university. The streets were blocked with burning tyres and the marks on the roads told me there were huge demonstrations taking place. I came back home to find many of my neighbours outside. They all looked troubled. Sirens could be heard in the distance and everyone in the street could see smoke. I looked around and saw the fear in people's faces. This time, I was old enough to understand that look on Um Hadi's face, whose child was still at school, or the way Um Amer looked as she waited for her husband who had not yet returned from work. They were not only confused but terrified of the unknown.

As we stood outside while the sun set, we suddenly heard a scream coming from the street. We rushed to see what was happening and found everyone looking at the sky. I looked but saw nothing. A minute later, I saw it: A flash of light passing so quickly, I thought it was a shooting star. After the third time, it was easy to recognise them as missiles being fired at us. People were still clapping and whistling, I don't know whether they thought they were fireworks or what. They did sound a bit like fireworks, but then there was the sound of a helicopter. We looked up but could not see anything. The sound was close but there was no sign of it in the smoky sky. Suddenly the power was out and the whole camp plunged into darkness. As everything became pitch black, we saw a flash of light in the sky, passing quickly to be replaced by a loud bang. I knew then that the helicopter had fired a missile and was surprised at how close the sound of the explosion was. We knew the missile had hit its target because the second sound, which followed shortly after, almost threw us to the ground. Everything was shaking as if a sudden earthquake had just hit the area. I didn't expect the second sound and my heart started to beat fast as I saw another flash in the sky. I crouched down again and covered my ears, but the sound was closer this time and almost pierced my ears. I stood up after the second sound and looked ahead, I could see a big fire to the east of our house, where I knew El-Markaz was.

After the second explosion people realised what was happening. Children were crying and women were screaming. I looked down at the street and saw shadows of people running around in confusion. We were terrified. It was the first time in our lives that we had been exposed to missiles and bombings. There was chaos in the street with more people shouting and running. I couldn't tell whether people were just confused and frightened or whether the explosions were getting nearer to their houses. Mother and I rushed inside and sat in the living room, candle in the middle, walls shaking every time a missile exploded. There was gunfire then and the sound of people shouting.

The week after, in early October 2000, I received a phone call from Zoe telling me that she wanted to see me immediately. I rushed to her apartment not knowing what was happening, not remembering us arguing about anything recently. When I arrived, she was standing in the kitchen preparing a sandwich. The flat looked unusually tidy, almost spotless. She offered me half of her snack as she continued to spread the butter on the bread before putting on some feta cheese and cucumber.

"I have something to tell you Omar," she said as she continued preparing her snack.

"I'm all ears."

"I am leaving today. I have packed all my things. A taxi is coming to take me to Erez at 4pm, I will go to Tel Aviv tonight and fly to London tomorrow." She waited for me to say something but

I could only stare at her. She could not meet my eyes. "I am sorry."

"Why? Where is this coming from?" I was not expecting this.

"It's time to go. I can't stay here any longer. My family are worried about me and they want me to go back."

"You could have told me earlier. We could have talked about it, spent more time together. You are leaving? Just like that, with no prior warning. You had a good time here and now that is it, you are leaving everything behind? Let the locals suffer, they are used to it?"

"Don't. Don't talk to me like that. Please. My parents are asking me to go back and I don't want to upset them. They want me with them. I just didn't want to upset you before, I know you have a lot on your plate."

She came close and hugged me, then looked into my eyes.

"Come with me. Come to London. I will sort out an invitation letter for you to get a visa. Let's live in peace for a while. Let's see who we really are."

I looked at her beautiful face, full of hope and excitement, but I was hurt that she had not told me she was leaving Gaza. That she was leaving me.

"This is my home and this is my place," I told her. "I will not go anywhere. It is your choice to leave, so go ahead."

I felt terrible trying to make her feel guilty. She had seemed genuine when she asked me to go. And who could blame her for going? She was frightened. Despite being so politically conscious, the rough life of Gaza did not suit her. Perhaps in "peace" times she had felt safe, but with the sound of the bombings and gunfire filling the streets, it was too much for her. She had tried to be a normal girlfriend, but in this place, there was no such thing as 'normal'.

I looked at her and imagined her in London with less conservative clothes, showing her pretty legs down the streets, European men chasing her. In that moment, I realised that I had completely forgotten that in the end, we were from different worlds. She was the English rose and I was that Palestinian kid who had seen nothing around him but destruction; no playground to go to, no alcohol to drink or night clubs to hang out at. In that brief moment, I realised that the chasm between us was unbridgeable. It was time to let her go and get back to who I really was: A Palestinian corpse in waiting. "We will talk, I promise. We will meet again."

We kissed for what seemed like an eternity. I opened the door and started descending downstairs, glancing back to look at her once more, watching as the tears started to fall down her cheeks. She looked so beautiful, I almost wanted to rush back and beg her not to leave. I continued down the stairs and out through the front door. I was gone, and so was she.

I wanted to shout down the street and curse my wretched life. I was angry with the Israelis but equally angry with my fellow Palestinians for throwing stones and shoes at the soldiers. I just wanted everyone to stop so I could rewind everything a couple of weeks to spend more time with Zoe. It was only then that I realised I was in love with her, and that I would miss her terribly when she was gone. But there was no hope for us now. She was my safety net, the person who lusted after me, the person who admired everything I did, including my stupid mistakes. She was clever and had such a presence. I could see the two of us being the trendiest couple ever. But that did not last long. All because of bloody politics.

The situation continued to go from bad to worse with more bombings and killings and no sign of a ceasefire, despite all the meetings politicians had. We had never experienced such aggression before. We thought the last *Intifada* was aggressive enough, but this one was a on a different level. We had never been attacked by helicopters and F-16s before and never seen what a single missile could do.

Given that police stations were constantly targeted by Israeli war jets, some prisoners at El-Abbas Prison were transferred to our headquarters in Tel El-Hawa and Khayyam was one of them. Issam asked me to oversee the transfer of prisoners to make sure that there was enough room for everyone and send the rest to other prisons in the south of the Gaza Strip. In February 2001, I saw Khayyam get out of a police truck in the middle of the courtyard of our centre.

I radioed the officer in charge immediately and asked him to bring him to my office. He looked terrified when he arrived.

"I told you I would bring you here eventually, and here you are. Now shall we do this the easy way or the nasty way?"

"Please," he begged as he looked at me in desperation, "look what is happening around you. We are being attacked left right and centre. This damn place could be bombed any minute and you are picking on me. Why don't you point your gun towards the Israelis who are killing us instead?"

"It seems like you've chosen the hard way then?" I went across the room and opened the drawer and pulled out my gun.

"No, please. Look, I don't know much, I swear. I only remember your father coming to me because he wanted to transfer ownership of the house to your mother. He said that he was worried that someone in the family might try to take it. That was in 1979 or 1980, if I remember correctly. At the time he did not have any children and he wanted ownership to go to his wife. We started preparing the paperwork for him to sign and I asked him to provide some bills. The next step would have been for both your parents to come to the office and sign all the legal documents. But that never happened because we never heard from your father again. We wrote to him several times asking for the completion of the paperwork and our fee, but we never heard back. Instead, we received a letter from your Uncle Attiya telling us that your father had disappeared and that he wanted to stop the transfer of ownership of the house to your mother. We wrote back to him saying that we had to wait for further instruction from his brother and that the transfer of ownership had not taken place because legal documents had not been signed. That is all that happened, I swear."

"Do you know where my father is now?" I asked in a low voice, hoping he would be able to say more.

"No, I swear."

"And this is all you can tell me?"

He looked at me for a second. "I don't know anything else. I wondered myself what happened to him, but then when the first *Intifada* started our firm closed and I moved to Egypt. I only returned to this damn city when the Palestinian Authority came to Gaza. I hoped that things would have changed and people would have forgotten everything. I did find it weird that your father never came back to us, but then I thought maybe the brothers had a fight and something happened. I could see why your uncle would object. Maybe he had hoped to inherit the house. You know what it is like when it comes to inheritance. People are very protective of their properties and family name associated with it. My guess is that your uncle did not want to see the transfer of the house to your mother, who comes from a different family. I have seen many cases like this; some of them were really bad and resulted in the death of family members. A client of mine killed his father because they wanted to write the house under the name of the older brother only. So I wasn't too surprised when I did not hear from your father and we never followed up. From our perspective nothing had happened and we could not get our fees back. We had other things on our minds."

"Like selling people's houses in their originals towns and villages," I said sarcastically.

"Don't start this, you know nothing about this matter, which will be decided in court."

I stared at him for a long time hoping that he would continue.

"Is there anything you want to tell me?" I said.

"No… wait, one more thing. I am not sure if this will interest you, but not long after your father disappeared, a man in a mask and crutches came to enquire about the house."

My eyebrows were raised by this. Mr. Khalil? Why would my geography teacher be interested in these things? Noticing I was interested, the prisoner continued.

"We refused to give him any information, of course, because it was confidential, He insisted and pulled out a gun, threatening to shoot me and my assistant. We told him that the transfer had not happened and then he took all the papers with him. We never saw him again."

I called for the soldier outside my office and asked him to take the solicitor back to his cell. Then I got my gun out, loaded it with ten bullets and left the office. I went out in the main street and flagged down a taxi to take me home. En route I phoned Ahmed and told him everything I had learned.

"I am convinced Uncle put my father in prison in order to get the house. It explains everything. All these years that he had been horrible to me was because he was disappointed that I was born and that there might be a chance of me inheriting the house. He wanted it for himself and his children." I was shouting now, sitting on the front passenger seat in the taxi as the driver glanced at me from time to time.

"Calm down a bit," Ahmed said, "let's just talk this through some more."

"I am going home right now to put a gun to his head. He will tell me the truth or I will blow his head to pieces. I have had enough, Ahmed, no more lying."

"Omar no, wait a bit, let me see you first."

I hung up and shouted at the driver to hurry up. I could not wait to get home and confront Uncle with everything I knew. There were lots of bombings that day with more police stations being attacked. There was black smoke in the air, making the usual fresh air of spring smell toxic.

Um Marwan was sitting in her usual place when I arrived. I jumped out of the taxi and threw his fare on the seat. He drove away quickly, calling me crazy. The car sped off, I ran towards my house, gun in hand, as Um Marwan stood up and shouted at me.

"Is everything OK? Omar? Omar... Wait!"

But I did not stop. I carried on running to our house. Mother was frightened of the look on my face and at seeing the gun.

"What happened?" She asked shakily.

"You need to come with me right now."

"Where to?"

"Uncle's house."

"But I am tired. I am not very well. Why can't you bring him here?"

"You have to get up right now, Mother. There is no more waiting and there is no more lying."

I pulled her by the headscarf as she sat on the chair next to the TV, ignoring her shout of pain. I dragged her all the way to the door, not stopping to even let her put her shoes on, as she continued to protest. Um Marwan saw me drag Mother out into the street and shouted at me again, asking what was happening, watching us walk around the corner and knock violently on Uncle's house.

Khalid opened the door and pointed for us to come in.

"I was just on my way out," he told us as he passed us.

"Where is Uncle?"

"In the TV room. Is everything all right?"

"Everything is fine. Just here to see Uncle."

Uncle was sitting alone on a mattress in the TV room. He was watching a news update on the number of martyrs created by this *Intifada*. He was wearing a very tight shirt and one of the buttons was missing, showing his hairy belly. I threw Mother on the mattress next to him and stepped back so they could both see me.

"Omar, what the hell are you doing throwing your mother around like that, have you no manners?"

She was silent and looked at him in despair.

"Funny, I would say she was the one with no manners, lying to me all these years. Just like you, Uncle Protector."

I pulled the gun out of the back of my trousers and pointed it at them.

"Omar what are you doing? Have you gone mad?" Mother screamed as she started crying.

"I want you to tell me the truth about Father right now, otherwise I swear by almighty God I will blow both your heads off right now."

I loaded my gun and put my finger on the trigger. Both remained silent.

"Tell me everything!"

Their silence had pushed me past frustration. I grew more and more angry as I thought of how they had lied for so long. All the troubles I had gone through, while they knew everything; all the abuse I received, all the people that had died because of me and all because they had refused to tell me the truth. At that point, I was ready to shoot even before they spoke. I truly felt I could have shot my own mother and not felt guilty about it. Instead I went to Uncle, who was still sitting on the mattress.

'"You wanted the house? Take this instead."

I hit him on the head with the back of my gun. He collapsed on the mattress, blood sliding down his head like a tiny snake. I kicked him hard in the stomach with my military boots. He tried to stand up but I put the gun to his face. His eyes begged me not to shoot him but I was ready to do it.

"You wanted the house for yourself so you hatched a plan to put my father in an Israeli prison and take everything for yourself. But it did not work out so well for you. I was born and spoiled the whole plan. Is this why you never liked me? Is this why you beat me? Because I spoiled your plan?" I looked at Mother. "And you! You never told me anything! Why? Did he frighten you? Do you know what I have gone through to try and find Father?"

"Your father made mistakes!" Uncle shouted at me.

I turned back to him and pointed the gun at his face, ready to shoot him. At that moment Um Marwan came through the door, followed by Ahmed.

"What mistakes? That he wanted to transfer the house to Mother's name? Is that a mistake important enough to make you get rid of your own brother? Is the property more valuable than his life? Did it not mean anything to you?"

I was crying as I said this and hit him again with the back of the gun on his nose. He screamed with pain. Mother was crying uncontrollably. Um Marwan and Ahmed started shouting at me to put the gun down. Ahmed even tried to get close to me to take it from me but I pointed it to his face. I had lost my mind.

"Omar, do not do this. Let the law get you your justice." He was moving slowly towards me, his hands reaching out to me. "Put your gun down my friend. I beg you not to waste your life or future on him. He is not worth it."

I was beyond reasoning with. I moved back towards Uncle who was now lying flat on his stomach on the mattress, blood all over his head and face. Mother's blue dress was already stained with some of it. I bent down and put my knee on his back and lowered my gun right to his head. I was breathing heavily. Everyone was silent, except for Uncle who was letting out small moans of pain. I had made my mind up; he should die and end all this suffering.

"It was not him, it was her!"

I turned around to see Um Marwan and saw her point at Mother.

"What are you talking about?"

"She was the one who put your father in prison, not him."

"What?" I did not understand. My eyes were getting hazy. I

was losing my mind completely. Mother just sat there and did not say a word.

"Is this some sort of game to mess with my head?" I shouted at her as I got off Uncle's back.

"It is the truth, Omar."

"What truth? What truth have you just decided to tell me now? What truth that I nearly killed for? What truth? Tell me."

Ahmed was silent, staring at me the whole time. Neither of us had expected this; my own mother responsible for the disappearance of my father.

Mother sat there on the mattress, looking away with tears running down her cheeks. Um Marwan sat down too. I stood holding my gun, looking around the room, not knowing what to do next.

"Speak up," I said finally, as I pointed the gun towards Um Marwan.

17

"She was the one who put him in prison," Um Marwan said. "That was why she married him in the first place – to spy on Mustafa and his men. Your father was the leader of the resistance movement in the north of the Gaza Strip. In fact, he was one of the founders of the Fatah resistance movement with a bunch of people who all ended up either killed or imprisoned because of her. Attiya discovered this on the night his brother disappeared. He went to tell your father what he had suspected for a long time and to prove the whole marriage was a set-up to try and get as much information out of him as possible. But Mustafa refused to believe this. He left the house in anger and slammed the door behind him, and that was the last time we saw him. We learned that he had been arrested a couple of hours later. The Israelis got wind of the fact that their informant had been discovered and decided to arrest your father.

"He was too naïve and loved this woman too much to believe that she could do anything to harm him. He admired her strong personality, the rebellion that she led against all social customs. Your father was a rebel himself. He did not like the way men treated women in this country. He found it refreshing that Souad was different; that she was not ashamed of being a woman and that she behaved like she was equal to him. He was blind to everything else that was going around him.

"You see, the Israelis knew about your father and the fact that he established Fatah here, which had connections and direct communication with the leadership of the party in Lebanon, and specifically with Yasser Arafat himself. They did not just want to arrest or kill Mustafa, they wanted to find out as much information as possible about everyone involved – what sort of communication was taking place with the leadership abroad, planned military attacks on Israeli targets both in Gaza and the south of Lebanon where the resistance was very active. So, they decided to send their best agent to do the job. When your grandfather went to ask for her hand in marriage, she said to her father that Mustafa was the one she had been waiting for. What she didn't say was the missing part of the sentence 'as instructed by my boss, Yitzhak' the infamous Israeli soldier who later became the loathed governor at El-Markaz, before Uri came to replace him.

"Your mother refused to adhere to our social norms, which we inherited through generations. When she was a teenager she insisted on wearing miniskirts, running away from school, smoking on the beach and sometimes even taking some hash. She was a teenager with a rebellious spirit, which shaped everything she did. At the age of seventeen she knew all about the feminist movement in Palestine and argued for a strong women's front, which would contribute effectively to the national cause. She believed that society needed its two halves to be functional together, in order to achieve freedom; if one was missing then there was no point of asking for liberation. First we needed to be liberated from within. All of these were valid points of course, and we all applaud them. I, myself, advocate them all the time. However, your mother's ego grew bigger as she rebelled against every social norm, sometimes just for the sake of rebelling rather than anything else.

"One day, when she skipped school with some friends and went to the hill by Deir El-Balah, where they normally met to smoke, an Israeli jeep discovered them. The soldiers got out and started smoking with the girls. After all, they were all teenagers except for one, Yitzhak, who had a different plan altogether. He asked Souad to walk with him on the beach and when they got there, he got out a bottle of whisky and offered her some. Being the rebel she was, she took a couple of swigs from the bottle and it went straight to her head. Eventually the inevitable happened and they kissed, which led to them having sex on the beach.

"She realised that she had made a terrible mistake as soon as it was over and stumbled home as quickly as possible, leaving Yitzhak behind and hoping that this would be the last time she would see him. But Yitzhak turned up at her house the next morning and asked your grandfather permission to speak to her alone. He told her she could collaborate with the Israeli army or she could refuse and he would tell the neighbourhood everything about the day before, which would be a death sentence. She would have never been able to fight her people's judgement and the abuse she would receive from them, not only for having sex outside wedlock, but with an Israeli soldier.

"She collaborated with them for a long time, at least six years, until orders came from Lieutenant Yitzhak to wait for someone called Mustafa Ouda, who was coming to ask for her hand in marriage. She had already refused several marriage proposals, preferring not to drag other people into the mess. But Yitzhak had got to her."

At that point Um Marwan paused and looked at Mother who was soaked in tears. My own Mother was a collaborator and had slept with an Israeli soldier. My own Mother married my father because of an order, rather than love. I knelt down, lifting her head up.

"Why? Why did you do that?" I asked.

"Every time I went to his office in Khan Younis to tell him that I could not collaborate anymore, he abused me and often raped me. I did not want to do this, but I couldn't get out of it, I was dead either way," she shouted back at me.

But then she pushed my hand away and started screaming, sobbing so loudly and hitting the mattress with her fist. She was so hysterical that Ahmed shouted at me to stop, but I was not going to. I had lived my entire life for that moment; to know the truth, the entire truth and not snippets. I was determined that no one would walk out of there without telling me everything they knew. Uncle Attiya was sitting up, his back leaning against the wall.

"Carry on," I nodded at Um Marwan, knowing that Mother wasn't in the state to tell me everything.

"So she married Mustafa, whose father was advised by another collaborator in the camp to go and ask for the girl's hand. You know how things were like then, that was how people got married. Call it arranged marriage or whatever, but it was upon the recommendation of people. When your grandfather and Mustafa saw the girl, they immediately fell in love with her. She was beautiful, charming, and clever. She came to offer them tea without the headscarf on. That day, when we went to ask for her hand, we were shocked at the sight of her. People were conservative about these things, but not your mother. It was what made your father more determined to marry her. He told his father that he was looking for a woman, who could think for herself; who could be an equal to him. He was not interested in having a slave in the house. You see Mustafa was building the national resistance movement with his men and my guess was that he wanted to involve her at some point. Little did he know about her being already involved.

"It was this man, your uncle, who discovered everything. One dark night in 1980, he woke up and noticed the flashlights of the Israeli military jeeps outside his window. There was a curfew that day and no one was allowed to go out. He looked out of his window and saw that the Israeli soldiers were spraying graffiti over your father's newly cleaned wall. He knew that there was no graffiti on the wall, before as the whole neighbourhood had cleaned their walls hoping for a quiet night. He was intrigued to see that the soldiers were the ones who were doing the graffiti themselves. Five minutes later, your father was brought out of the house pushed by the soldiers and ordered to clean. He did so with a smile on his face and in the same manner he always did. The next morning, Attiya asked me if I had ever noticed anything similar happen. We talked about it, both puzzled and we decided to keep a watch on what was happening.

"This happened a number of times, while either Attiya or myself stayed on night watch to see whether the soldiers were spraying the graffiti. They did it at least once a week. On all the occasions we witnessed, only your father's wall was sprayed by the soldiers who then asked him to clean it. But one more interesting thing we noticed was that Yitzhak, now promoted to governor of El-Markaz, was always there too.

"Attiya started recording all those patterns. He knew that your father was an important figure in the resistance despite the fact that no one else in the street knew, Mustafa being very careful with the times he chose to leave the house and the disguise he put on. He always wore extra high-heeled boots when he was coming in and out of the house. He also tucked a *kufiyyah* under his shirt to make him look fat. Surprisingly enough this worked, as people made quick judgements when they saw a tall fat figure in the shadows of the night. They never suspected it was your father. But I knew because I saw him come in and out of the house. Attiya knew because he often watched his back, making sure that there was no one in the street.

"Attiya and I got together one day and made a list of all the people who were either killed or arrested recently in the Jabalia Camp, and discovered that they were all connected to Mustafa. We concluded that there was an informant within the circle that is giving away information. Your uncle got worried about his brother and tried to warn him a few times. But we discovered the horrible truth ourselves not that much later.

"Attiya was caught up in the curfew that night, but he was determined to go home, despite the gunfire that he could hear from his friend's house. He was worried about your father and wanted to get there as soon as possible. There was a lot of fighting that evening as he dodged his way in the dark alleys of the Jabalia Camp. To his horror, he stumbled across an injured masked man who was bleeding very badly. When Attiya removed his mask, he recognised Osama Ridwan. He was your father's right-hand man. Osama was convinced that either your father or your mother was the informant, because no one else knew about the operation except the three of them. He died later in that same alley.

"Attiya went straight to your father's house to confront him, but Mustafa refused to believe what his brother had to say. He left the house in anger. When he did not show up late that morning, Attiya went back to your house with a knife in his hand. I rushed in just in time to see him put the knife to your mother's throat. She confessed everything to us. She told us your father had already been arrested that morning, given that the whole scheme had then been discovered. Attiya was about to stab her to death had it not been for you; I reminded him that a six-month-old baby needed his mother beside him. You looked like a little angel in your sleep. She told us how she passed the information to Yitzhak during the graffiti-cleaning sessions, when your father was outside with the soldiers, and the governor stayed in the house questioning her, sometimes even raping her if she did not have enough information."

I stared at Mother, the person who had been everything to me. She looked almost a hundred years old as she crouched into a ball on the small mattress, unable to speak and shaking violently. The person who had been my goddess was the one who betrayed me and Father, the reason for all this misery, the reason I was abused, caused death to others. We had both betrayed the people around us. We were both spies; collaborating with the enemy and abused when we refused to. I almost wanted to go to her and comfort her – tell her that I understood. But I, at least, had tried to fight. I had finally been brave enough to face the resistance. Even to tell Zoe.

The woman whom I once thought the bravest in the world turned out to be a coward, who had married someone who loved her so much and gave her everything, only to get him arrested.

"They did not need her anymore," Um Marwan carried on. "After your father had been arrested and most of his group had either been arrested or killed, they threw her away and did not care what fate she would face. Attiya and I knew that you would need her. You needed a mother to look after you; none of this was your fault. But we had to keep a close eye on her for a long time, until we made sure that there was no contact between her and the Israelis anymore. When Yitzhak was moved to the West Bank and Uri took over, she was asked to go to El-Markaz to meet the new governor. But your uncle insisted on accompanying her. He waited outside until she came out with her discharge paper from the Mossad and a few hundred dollars as a reward to her service.

"Your uncle immediately took over your father's position in the resistance, partly because of his anger towards the Israelis and partly because he wanted to keep an eye on Souad, and you for that matter. You see, he was the one who fired that shot when you got caught up in the curfew while trying to go to Ahmed's house. The one who whispered to the leader of the resistance group that you would be used as a double agent rather than be killed – which they were about to do when I took you to them. He was the one who watched you closely every time Uri took you to El-Markaz, he was the one who demanded that Abu Hammad, the finest man in this Strip, should stay with you."

I stared at my uncle who looked up towards me as he leaned against the wall. His eyes were watering. I looked down at his tight shirt and his belly and suddenly I understood everything. How blind I was not to have figured this out before. His blood was still dripping from his neck.

"I am sorry," he said in a barely audible voice.

"What difference does your apology make? Why couldn't you have told me before?"

"I was going to tell you, I swear, but maybe when you grew older or when..."

"But you knew all along that I was a collaborator, you knew everything, and you did nothing to help."

"I didn't know you were an informant, I thought you were just on the trail of finding your father. I was shocked when Um Marwan brought you to the resistance."

Ahmed was glaring at me, his teeth clenched together in anger.

"You were a spy?" He shouted as Mother looked up from her crouching position.

"Apparently it runs in the family."

I explained everything. I recounted every single minute of the horror I had been through, as my friend wept. When I got to the part where Uri took my trousers off, Mother flinched as if feeling it herself. Um Marwan wept too, as Uncle Attiya looked wretched.

"What about the house and Mr. Khayyam El-Farra?" I asked, looking at Uncle.

"Your father wanted to transfer the property to your mother, but when we found out everything we needed to make sure that this would not happen and that the property would be in your name, you being the rightful heir. But as your father was still the owner, unable to go back to sign the papers, by default you were the heir in case anything happened to him."

"But what about Mr. Khalil? Why was he asking about the papers?"

Uncle and Um Marwan shared an apprehensive look, but it was Mother who finally broke the silence.

"We wanted to run away. We wanted to leave this damn place

and never come back again. We wanted to sell thc house and maybe go to Egypt and start all over again and never come back, never, NEVER..." She was getting more and more hysterical, beating herself and slapping her cheeks.

I looked at that selfish woman who didn't care about her son and was only interested in starting again and making things better for herself, rather than fixing the mess that she got everyone involved in. Uncle and Um Marwan were watching without saying a word. Ahmed came close to me and gave me a big hug, as she continued to shout. I wanted to run up to her and shoot her and end all of this.

My own mother was the worst enemy I had, the person I had trusted to prepare my food, to wash me in the shower, to switch the light off in my room every night, to tell me bedtime stories, to smile, play and watch TV with. I was nothing but one of the mistakes she had made in her life. I wished that, despite all her mistakes, my birth was the one that she had not made.

I thought of Mr. Khalil and where he would be now, feeling stupid for letting him go that night. He had known everything too and never told me anything. Instead, he was planning an escape with Mother, leaving me behind with Uncle. They wanted to sell the house that my own father built to go and have a good time in Egypt. I thought about the night I let Khalil go and wished I had left him there in his house, waiting for the bullets of the resistance.

"What about Father, where is he now?" My voice was shaking, unable to bear much more.

"He is in the Beer Sheva Prison," Uncle Attiya answered. "I have visited him many times, but not since the Palestinian Authority came. Now, with this second *Intifada*, we are not allowed to visit relatives in Israeli prisons."

"Will I be able to see him?"

"*Inshallah*, one day my son."

It was the first time in my life that I liked Uncle calling me that and wanted him to say it again. I wanted to be a child again, to rewind everything to spend more time with him and let him treat me as his own child, as he always intended to.

18

I couldn't stay in that house anymore. That night, Ahmed let me stay in his place. We ate dinner in silence, while Soumaya and Abu Ahmed watched us carefully. The four of us just chewed our hummus and falafel in silence. I thought about Mother. She had never wanted me and she had never loved anyone. She may have played some motherly role and looked after me out of duty, but as I sat there watching Ahmed and his family, I wondered how much of that was out of her own love or the threats of my guardian uncle. Would she have gotten rid of me if Uncle Attiya had not been there to make it difficult for her to do so? There were lots of questions that I wanted to ask her, but the reality was I could not see her anymore, and perhaps I did not want to find out any more of the truth.

The next couple of weeks were haunted with silence at home. Mother and I did not talk at all. I made sure to leave first thing in the morning and come back really late, after she had gone to bed. From time to time, I heard her cry in the room and shout at me to come and talk to her, but I could not. We were two prisoners, trapped in our own mistakes and guilt. It pained me so much to hear her cry. In some ways, I wanted to go and silence her forever, but it rather killed me to see and hear her in that state. To see the proud, strong woman I had always known locking herself up in a small room, like an old wounded beast who was then unable to do anything but watch people stare at it with pity. I finally came to understand the way Um Marwan always looked at Mother and why she refused to come to our house. She felt sorry for her and wanted to avoid the humiliation of coming to our house. She wanted that beast to stay on its own and away from everybody else.

Two weeks later, I moved to a small studio apartment in the El-Ansar area in Gaza City, overlooking the sea. It took great courage to make that decision, knowing how ill Mother was, but the whole thing had become too much for me to handle. Ahmed too thought it was good for me, provided that I would check on Mother. He promised to help and make sure to drop by regularly to check that there was enough food in the house. I hired a cleaner to come three times a week and I dropped by every Friday, opened the door in the morning and went straight to the kitchen to prepare food. I would then go to the mosque and, when I got back, we just sat in the TV room and ate in silence. We did not exchange a single word or, worse, a look.

In 2002, both Ahmed and I graduated from university. I got a 2:1 degree in English Literature while Ahmed finished with a distinction in his BSc in Business and Commerce. We were both happy and went out to a restaurant to celebrate. I wanted Father to be with me more than at any time, to see his own son graduating and becoming a man. Work at the Preventive Security Forces was getting more difficult with all the bombings and attacks that Israel continued to rain on us from their jet planes. They sent us home most of the time, which I did not mind as it gave me the opportunity to focus more on my university work, hence managing to pass with a good grade.

It was on the evening that we went for dinner on Gaza beach that I received a call from Uncle telling me that Mother had been taken to hospital. She had cut her wrists with a kitchen knife and had lost a lot of blood. I left everyone at the table and rushed to

El-Awda Hospital in the Jabalia Camp. When I arrived there, Khalid was smoking a cigarette outside the hospital. He told me which floor she was on and I rushed up the stairs, not waiting for an elevator. Uncle and his wife were outside the operating room. They had a very worried look on their faces.

We waited in silence for hours. I spoke to Ahmed a few times, giving him an update on the progress. To my surprise I also received a call from Zoe around midnight. She was a little tipsy and told me how much she missed me. She cried when I told her that I was in hospital with Mother and that I needed to speak to her another time. She promised to call in the morning. When I hung up, the surgeon had already emerged out of the theatre.

"*Allah akhad wadeito*, God has taken back his deposit," he said as he was shook his head. "I am sorry. We did our best but she had already lost too much blood. May Allah bless her soul. I am sure you will meet in heaven."

Uncle's wife was crying already. He held her with his two big strong arms and rested his chin on her head. I leaned back against the wall and just stared. Everything became a blur, as if someone had slowed time down. I could see shapes of things moving but did not really know what they were or where they were going. I came back to reality when the doctor came up to me and asked me to sign a paper, which I did without even reading. I walked into the room, worried about the sight that I would see. She was lying on the big, silver table, covered up to the head with a hospital blanket. Her bare feet were showing at the other end. I walked straight to her head and uncovered her face.

I stood by her head and stared at that face which I used to look up to. I thought of how selfish she was to take her life like that. We had been separated a few months and did not speak at all, but she was my mother; the one who gave me life, the one I loved for a long time, the one who was my idol. Suddenly, I felt guilty for not being there for her and for allowing such a thing to happen. I realised that I had hardly known her and felt sorry for not trying to reach out to her before. I remembered the day I discovered that she wore glasses and cursed myself for never really asking her questions or never really truly getting to know her. But she had chosen this; this was what she wanted. She wanted to die. Suddenly, all my anger left me. I had no right to be angry with her. She made lots of mistakes, but she was gone. I cried, sobbing like a lost child. I fell on my knees, kissing her hand and wailing. When it came to it, when she was really gone, I felt the emptiness around me like a ghost that would haunt me for the rest of my days.

Zoe and I spoke several times after the funeral. She was very supportive and offered to come to Gaza again to spend some time with me, which I appreciated but refused. I wanted some time on my own. A few months after Mother had passed away, I quit my job at the Preventive Security Forces, much to Issam's dismay, who did his best to convince me to stay, promising further promotions and salary increases. I could not do it anymore. I wanted to be a normal person. I learnt not to speak or even think about Father, who was, for now, completely out of reach. I got a job as a translator in a small firm on El-Nasr Street in Gaza City. Ahmed and I continued to see each other regularly and I moved back home to the Jabalia Camp, so I could be closer to him and Uncle. I was pleased to hear that Ahmed got engaged to a beautiful girl who worked with him at the branch of the Arab Bank in Gaza.

In November 2004, Yasser Arafat passed away in Paris under strange circumstances. We all watched the announcement on TV with great sadness. It was that day that I realised there was no hope left for the Gaza Strip and that I had to go. I had to leave all this sadness behind and start over somewhere else. I spoke to Zoe and discussed going to London. I wanted to go somewhere to pursue my dream of studying for a Masters degree and becoming a successful academic. She helped me apply to several universities in London and I got my offer in May 2005.

It took six more months for me to get the visa to enter the UK, which arrived on 25 January 2006, the very same day it was announced that Hamas had won the Palestinian elections.

That was the same day that I told Ahmed and Uncle about my plans to leave; I called them both and asked them to come over after I had picked up my visa from El-Riyadh Tower in Gaza City, where the British Consulate Office was. They were both waiting for me outside my door when I arrived. I made tea as they chatted about the news of the day and what was going to happen after Hamas won the elections. People expected everyone to refuse the results and to force the conservative party out of government. Uncle was optimistic that some sort of unity government deal could be struck between Hamas and Fatah. Finally, I turned the TV off.

"I am leaving Gaza. I got my visa for London today." "What?" Ahmed exclaimed, completely shocked. "When did that happen?"

"I have been talking with Zoe about it for a while now, and I feel it is time to move on. There is nothing left for me here."

"What about us?" Ahmed insisted. "What about your uncle and your father?"

"Father is never going to be released from prison and now that Hamas is in government I doubt things will change and I will be allowed to visit him," I replied bitterly.

We fell into silence for a few minutes, as I let them digest this piece of news.

"Will you have enough money to pay for your studies?" Uncle finally asked.

"I have got some but I will try to get a part-time job to help me out."

Ahmed continued to shower me with questions about the details of the move that I had not yet thought through myself, as if he was trying to put me off the idea. I wanted him to just shut up, but I understood how angry he was with me that I had not even discussed the plans with him. I looked at my friend and wanted to smile, watching his passionate face as he fired more questions at me. If it hadn't been for that passionate face, things would have been different; I might not even be there now.

The night before I left, all my friends and neighbours came to say goodbye. The house was full of people, cousins of the extended Ouda family, old friends from school, teachers, neighbours; it looked as though a demonstration was about to start. The only people missing were my parents. I sat in the middle of a big circle telling everyone about my plans and making promises to keep in touch with them all. Abu Ahmed took $100 out of his pockets and stuffed it in mine, saying that I would need it while I was there.

In the morning, a queue of neighbours stood outside the house. I shook hands with all of them until I got to Uncle. I looked straight into his eyes, wondering what would happen to me in this new world without my protector. He hugged me tight.

"You will be just fine, son. Don't worry about anything."

I handed him the key to my house, the legal papers and the key for the old flattened house in Deir Snade. He was pleased and honoured to look after them, knowing that his brother would be very happy to know that they were still safe. I was heading to the car when I noticed that Um Marwan was not there. I rushed to her house and saw her stuck in her embroidery stacks, crying as she folded her work and organised them into different sacks. She could not stand up as I walked in, so I bent down and hugged her tightly, crying as we said our goodbyes. Finally ready to go, Ahmed, Khalid and I bundled into the car. As we left the Jabalia Camp, I could not force myself to look.

The car raced ahead and we were at the Rafah Border Crossing in no time. I got my bags and walked straight to the border without looking back or stopping to hug my friend and my cousin. I was too embarrassed to let them see me cry. I could feel their eyes on the back of my head, as if they understood that it was too much for me to say goodbye. But at the last minute, after I had got my passport back, I turned around and waved at them with a smile. I saw their smile too as they waved. Khalid tried to come forward to the main gate, but was stopped by a Palestinian policeman. I went through the Palestinian side with no problem until I got to the Egyptian side, where I was deported to Cairo on a scruffy old bus with 80 other people crammed in it. In Cairo, I was put in a basement room called 'the deportation room' and stayed there for five days, until my flight to London was about to leave.

Five months after I arrived in London, Hamas captured the Israeli soldier, Gilad Shalit, on the border of Gaza. The abduction took place in June 2006 and all hell broke loose. The crossing was shut permanently and I watched the bombardment of my Gaza Strip on TV while preparing to start my MA in English Literature at London Metropolitan University. When Hamas took over the Gaza Strip in May 2007 and became the ruling government, the siege was tightened completely and I knew that there would be no chance to go back anymore. I emailed Issam from London reminding him what I had said; that they would take over one day and that this peace agreement was going to turn us against each other. I never got a response from Issam – he was killed by Hamas fighters who had taken over Tel El-Hawa.

Not being able to go back actually helped me adapt to my new life in London. I was determined to finish my Masters, which I did, and then started a PhD at Goldsmiths College, University of London, in September 2007. I kept in touch with Ahmed and Uncle, phoning them every Saturday, the only day of the week I did not work. I had found a part-time job at a small theatre doing some marketing, in order to pay my bills.

Zoe and I got engaged in early 2008 and were married by the end of the year. We rented a small apartment near Hoxton Square to be close to her job at Amnesty International's head office in the city. Our wedding was a small affair attended only by a few Palestinians I had met in London and a handful of Zoe's family. When we arrived at our newly rented flat, I remembered the first time I went to her tiny place in Gaza City. We made love and hugged for a long time after. It felt good to be in her arms and to feel that life was starting again – differently. I was finally in control of my own life and determined to forget all the pains of the past and build a happy family in this new world. But at the end of 2008, my hopes were shattered after spending a lovely Christmas Day with Zoe's father. I switched the TV on and saw the news of one hundred Hamas policemen killed in one single attack. My heart dropped as I saw images of the Jabalia Camp being bombarded. I spoke to Ahmed and Uncle every day during those difficult three weeks. I woke up every morning with the fear that something might happen to them and wanting to go back to help them. But with the border shut I could not reach them. My horror intensified when I saw the El-Fakhoura School, where Ahmed and I had spent our early years in the first *Intifada*, being burned down with white phosphorous, released by Israeli planes. It was not until that moment that I realised that there was no going back to Gaza and even if I wanted to, it could all be burned down by the time I managed to get there.

Zoe and I had a small boy at the end of 2009, whom we named Mustafa after my father. He had dark brown hair and green eyes and olive skin. He became the joy of my life. I dreamt of the day that Mustafa and I would travel to Gaza to show him where his father grew up, to introduce him to Ahmed who by then had already had four children. But I was afraid to go back to Gaza and see what had befallen it.

In February 2011, Hosni Mubarak's regime in Egypt fell and a few months later the border was reopened. Even though I was full of enthusiasm, I refused to travel back immediately, making excuses to Zoe who was pushing me to go. She wanted to come with me too but I kept delaying and making excuses.

In September 2011, Hamas and Israel reached a prisoner exchange agreement to release the captured Israeli soldier, as Israel approved the release of 1,027 Palestinians. I watched the news with excitement, which quickly turned into fear; talking to Ahmed on the phone, I was informed that Father's name was on the list to be released. I wasn't sure I actually wanted to meet him after all these years. I was shaking. What would I say to him? Where would we start?

"You should come, Omar. It is the moment we have been waiting for," Uncle's voice was so loud on the phone.

"I am worried, Uncle." I did not know what to tell him and whether to admit that I would rather things were over and the past would not be disturbed again.

"You must Omar. He made mistakes, but he did not know things would end up the way they did. I beg you to come without delay."

"But what if we don't get along? We don't even know each other, Uncle."

"He is your father, Omar, the man you had been searching for all these years. If you do not come you will always wonder what it would have been like to wait for him at the Erez Crossing as he got off that bus."

Zoe hugged me goodbye at Heathrow as I went to board the plane. I gave little Mustafa a big hug and told them to wait for my call to come to Gaza, if the situation allowed. I had already asked her to contact the Egyptian embassy to start sorting out entry permission to the Gaza Strip. The Egyptians were keeping a tight watch on who entered Gaza, and anyone without permission would have to go through endless procedures.

My heart raced as I travelled out of Cairo and across the Suez Canal into the Sinai desert, back again on the familiar deportation bus. I finally arrived at the Egyptian side of the Rafah Crossing. I could see Gaza from the distance as the bus left El-Areesh and approached the Egyptian town of Sheikh Zoaid. I was glued to the window, remembering the first time I made the journey, leaving all the agony behind me and hoping for a better life. Now I was going back to meet the man who helped make me; the man I had never been able to call Father to his face. After a long messy queue on the Egyptian side, I was finally put on the bus to the Palestinian side of the crossing. The Palestinian police that watched the border were all Hamas. I was taken aback when the officer who took my passport asked me to go to a room for further questions. My own people were now questioning me for going back home. I was angry. An old man wearing a white *Jalabiya* and a long white beard entered and started asking me all sorts of questions about why I had left Gaza and why I had not been back since. But most importantly, they wanted to know whether I still had any links with Fatah and the leadership in Ramallah and the West Bank.

My salvation came from the most unexpected person. It was no other than Abu Hammad himself, walking across the room with a radio in his hand. I would never forget the face that had finally been revealed to me that night I let him go. His ginger hair and dark green eyes were unforgettable. We sat for a bit and he ordered a coffee for me. Apparently he had become a leader in the Qassam brigades and was in charge of their Interior Security Division. He was dressed up in a military suit and had a few stars and symbols on his shoulders. I gave him a quick update on my news and we agreed to meet again soon. As we embraced goodbye, I wondered again what the difference between us was. He was playing the same role I could have been playing, had things remained the way they were. It looked like a worthless position in a phantom government under tight Israeli occupation. We would both only govern and control our own people.

Uncle and Ahmed were waiting outside and they rushed towards me the moment they spotted me, hugging me and kissing me on the cheek. We headed to the taxi which was waiting by the main gate and drove to the Jabalia Camp as Ahmed gave me a guided tour of all the buildings that had been destroyed and the areas that had been flattened. Gaza looked strange and almost like a different place altogether. But despite all the destruction, despite all the misery that had resided in that place, there was some energy in people's faces. They continued to laugh and they continued to believe that one day they would be victorious and this whole nightmare would be over.

On Tuesday 18 October, Gilad Shalit, the captured Israeli soldier, was finally handed over to the Egyptian army as part of the exchange deal, and four buses carrying 350 Palestinian prisoners arrived at the Palestinian side of the Erez Crossing. I was there with Uncle. Mustafa Ouda, my own father, was confirmed to be on the last bus entering from Israel. We waited in the open space outside the crossing, among the cheers and shouts of all family members who had come to welcome their loved ones. Some were carrying pictures of their dead family members as if bringing their spirit to meet their freed family member. Uncle and I kept looking at each other in anticipation until the final bus finished unloading. There was still no Father to be seen. I was relying on Uncle's facial reactions as he surveyed all the faces coming out of the buses. There were times during that wait when I wanted to turn around and run away, go back to my safe life in London. Some part of me wanted him not to be on the bus. I did not know how to feel.

Uncle started to move towards the bus and I followed quickly. He was rushing as he saw the bus driver get out of the bus and open the side to get out what looked like a wheelchair. A moment later he went up and came back carrying an old, disabled Palestinian. Uncle was standing in front of the motionless man. I caught up with Uncle as he was bending down.

"Mustafa, it is me, Attiya. *Hamdellah ala es-salama.* Welcome home."

But there was no response. Uncle Attiya looked at me, his eyes already filled with tears. The man I had been waiting for all my life was sitting in a wheelchair unable to make a single gesture. I looked at his round face with the white stubble that had covered most of its features but did not hide the folds and wrinkles of years of suffering. I compared that face to the photo I had kept with me all this time; I could see the similarities in my mind but did not expect him to be that weak. I hugged him tightly as he continued to stare blankly ahead, as if no one was there.

As we remained there for a while, the driver came back down carrying a brown envelope that he handed to Uncle. He explained that it had all of Father's medical records; a stroke a couple of years ago had left him completely paralysed. I stood there looking at him as Uncle bent down and whispered in his ears words I could not hear. I looked at my father and wondered whether he even recognised me.

We went home. Ahmed and Abu Ahmed were the first well-wishers. Ahmed's father asked me about my life in London. I told him everything as we sat there in my old living room, wondering what it would have been like if Mother was still alive. Would Father have been able to come back home at all? The house was filled with guests, relatives and everyone in the streets who had come to have a look at the wounded lion whose reputation had spread across the Jabalia Camp: The leader of the resistance had been freed. Ahmed and I were playing host, constantly serving teas, coffees and coke to the influx of visitors who came while Uncle sat in the living room and greeted them all. Occasionally, he got up and wheeled father to the bathroom, staying there for a bit and then coming back. I caught a glimpse of him going into the bathroom and realised how much Uncle loved his brother. Watching them together, I could tell that there was a lot of happiness that had filled their lives as they had grown up together. This was why Uncle held on to Father and the hope that one day he would be able to see him.

She came late in the evening when everyone had left and

knocked on the door as Ahmed was preparing to leave and Uncle was getting sleepy. I opened the door for her and saw an old woman leaning on a walking stick, unable to move, back bent.

"Let me in," she said, "let me see him."

"Um Marwan? It's me, Omar."

She smiled at me and gave me a big hug, but all she really wanted was to pass me by to go to Father. The moment she spotted him across the room on his wheelchair, she dropped her walking stick and rushed to his side. She let out a cry of joy as she reached him and showered him with kisses and hugs. Um Marwan insisted on staying the night and ended up staying for most of the week. Somehow she got her strength back. She would wake up early in the morning and clean the house and prepare some breakfast. It was clear just how much she loved Father. She treated us both like sons while she stayed with us. But Father was silent all the time. He just continued to stare ahead as if no one was there.

I phoned Zoe and asked her to book herself a ticket on the next plane to Cairo and then take a taxi for the dreaded journey to Gaza. She arrived three days later, full of excitement to see Gaza again. I held my son Mustafa and brought him closer to Father.

"Look, Father. This is your grandson, Mustafa. He looks just like you." I spoke in a soft voice as Um Marwan stopped the noise she was making in the kitchen and Zoe came and gave me a big hug, holding my waist from the back.

"I would have liked things to be different and that you could have held him. In fact, I would have liked everything to be different, but that is not up to me to decide. All I want now is to know that you are happy."

The lack of response from Father killed me. Over the days I tried to study all his features and whether they would change with different emotions or not. I did not notice any difference.

Until one day, after a long walk on the beach and back to the Jabalia Camp, Zoe was tired of chasing little Mustafa around and carrying him on her shoulders while I wheeled father on the badly made roads in Gaza. We got home as Um Marwan prepared some food for us. She seemed to have moved to our house permanently. Zoe jumped to help as I went to switch the radio on. One of my favourite songs, *Ya Rayeh*, by Rashid Taha, was playing on the radio. I started dancing around as I held Mustafa in my hands, twirling him up in the air, then putting him down and shaking my hips and laughing out loud. Mustafa was also enjoying it, scurrying backwards and forwards almost as if he was trying to dance. I held hands with him and followed his little steps as he exclaimed proudly. Zoe came from the kitchen and joined us and so did Um Marwan. I turned the volume up and we were all dancing. We twisted, twirled, clapped and jumped. But as I turned around, I noticed it: I rushed to Father who was sitting towards the back of the room in his wheelchair, as one tear ran down his cheek.

The next day Uncle came to me and asked me how long I wanted to stay in Gaza for. He told me to go back to my life in London and that he was going to look after Father. I had to think hard about that and talked to Zoe that night. I did not want to leave Father on his own in Gaza, not after I had spent years trying to be with him. Yet, at the same time, Gaza was no place for Mustafa to grow up, while the siege was still on and basic goods were scarce. The next day I informed Uncle that we would be leaving the following week. But before we did, I got Um Marwan to take a family picture of me, Father, Zoe and Uncle holding Mustafa. I got it blown up and framed and hung it on the wall in the middle of the room. I also found a small photo of Mother that I placed carefully in the bottom right corner of the frame, so she could be in the photograph with us.